A seaquake was one of the most dreaded of undersea phenomena. The vast domes that a brilliant technology had conceived and built on the ocean floor could be protected from most of the natural phenomena found at such colossal depths, but a quake, a tremor in the ocean floor itself, if strong enough, could set up chain reaction pressures that would split and shatter the dome. Then the back-up systems served only to provide a little time—time for people, hopefully, to escape to another dome, or even to the surface.

Cadet Jim Eden, assigned to the Krakatoa Dome, was fully aware that it was built in a seaquake-prone area—as had been the scientists who designed the dome in the first place. It had been designed specifically to cope with the known force and frequency of tremors in that area.

But something was terribly wrong. The seaquakes were occurring with greater frequency and strength than anyone had calculated. And not only in the Krakatoa area.

It was Jim Eden's task to find out why.

*And don't miss*

UNDERSEA QUEST
UNDERSEA FLEET

*Available from Ballantine Books*

# UNDERSEA CITY

## Frederik Pohl
and
## Jack Williamson

BALLANTINE BOOKS • NEW YORK

An Intext Publisher

Copyright © 1958 by Frederik Pohl and Jack Williamson

SBN 345-02209-2-075

First printing: April, 1971

Cover art by Gino D'Achille

Printed in the United States of America

BALLANTINE BOOKS, INC.
101 Fifth Avenue, New York, N.Y. 10003

# CONTENTS

# Undersea City

# 1

## The Inside Drift

"Cadet Eden, ten-*hut*!"

I stopped at the edge of the deepwater pool and stiffened to attention. I had been playing sea-tennis with Bob Eskow in the pool courts on a hot Saturday afternoon. I had come out to adjust my oxygen lung—I could see Eskow still in the water, gliding restlessly back and forth as he waited for me—and the Cadet Captain's sharp order caught me just about to dive back in.

"Cadet Eden, as you were!" I relaxed slightly and turned.

With the Cadet Captain was the O.O.D. He said, "Report to the Commandant's office at thirteen hundred hours, Cadet Eden. Now carry on." He returned my salute and walked off with the Cadet Captain.

Bob Eskow poked his head out of the water, flipped back his mask and complained: "Come on, Jim, what's holding up the game?"

Then he caught sight of the Cadet Captain and the O.O.D. He whistled. "What did they want?"

"I don't know. I've got to report to the Commandant at thirteen hundred, that's all."

Eskow climbed out and sprawled on the edge of the deepwater pool beside me. He said seriously, "Maybe it's what Danthorpe was talking about."

"What's that?"

1

Eskow shook his head. "He just hints around. But it's something involving you and me—and him."

"Forget it," I advised him, and sat down. I took off the mask of my lung and rechecked the bubble valve. It had been sticking. I had fixed it, but there is one thing you learn in the Sub-Sea Fleet and that is to make *doubly* sure that every piece of undersea equipment is working perfectly. The deeps don't give you a second chance.

The Bermuda sun was hot on the back of my neck. We had marched a lot of miles under that sun, as cadets at the Sub-Sea Academy, but now we had lost the habit of it. We had been too long under deadly miles of black water, Bob Eskow and I. The sun was strange to us.

Not that we minded the sun. In spite of all the inventions that are conquering the sea—spreading domed cities across that dark, drowned desert that is stranger than Mars—no invention can ever take the place of the clean smell of natural air and the freedom of the wide surface horizon. Not for the first few days, anyhow.

Bob Eskow stood up. He looked around him at the bright green trees and the red-tiled roofs above the hot white beach; he looked out at the whitecaps flashing out on the surface of the sea; and he said what was in my mind.

"It's worth all the pearls in the Tonga Trench just to be back."

I knew how he felt.

The deep sea gets into your blood. There's a strain and a danger that you can never forget. There's the dark shape of death, always there, waiting outside a film of shining edenite that is thinner than tissue, waiting for you to pull the wrong switch or touch the wrong valve so that it can get in. It can smash a city dome like a peanut under a truck, or slice a man to ribbons with a white jet of slashing brine—

"Quit your daydreaming, you two!"

We looked up.

Another cadet was approaching us.

I hadn't met him, but I knew his name: Harley Danthorpe. The one Bob Eskow had just mentioned.

He was slender and a bit shorter than Bob. He wore his

sea-scarlet dress uniform with knife-edge creases; his hair slick down flat against his scalp.

I didn't like the expression on his face as Bob introduced us; he seemed to be sneering, "Jim," said Bob, "Harley Danthorpe is a transfer student, from down deep."

"And going back there," said Danthorpe. He flicked a speck of coral dust from his sleeve. "Along with you two," he mentioned.

Bob and I looked at each other. "What are you talking about, Danthorpe? The fall term's about to begin—"

Danthorpe shook his head. "We won't be here. The orders will be out this afternoon."

I looked hard at him. "You aren't kidding us? How do you know?"

He shrugged. "I've got the inside drift."

And something happened.

It happened to Bob as well as to me; I could feel it and I could see it in his eyes. I didn't like Danthorpe. I didn't know whether to believe him or not—but the rumor had done something to me. The dry tingle of the sun felt just as good as ever. The sky was still as blue and as high, and the island breeze was just as sweet.

But suddenly I was ready to go down deep again.

I asked: "Where to?"

He stretched and glanced at me and at Bob, then turned and looked out over the sea. "Why Krakatoa Dome," he said.

Bob said sharply: "Krakatoa?"

"That's right," nodded Danthorpe. He looked at Bob curiously. For that matter, so did I; suddenly Bob's face had seemed to turn a degree paler.

I said quickly, trying to divert Danthorpe's attention from whatever it was that was bothering Bob: "What are we supposed to be going to Krakatoa for?"

Danthorpe shrugged. "I've got the inside drift, but not about that," he admitted. "All I know is that we're going."

Krakatoa! I wanted to believe him. Right at that minute I wanted it more than anything in the world. Krakatoa Dome was one of the newest of the undersea cities. It stood near the brink of the Java Trough, south of the famous volcanic island in the Sunda Strait, three miles down.

I wanted to go there very much. But I couldn't believe that it was possible.

I knew something about Krakatoa Dome. My Uncle Stewart Eden had spoken many times of the wealth around it, the sea-floor rotten with oil, pocketed with uranium and precious tin. But I had never heard that the Sub-Sea Fleet had a training station there. And what other reason could there be for detaching three cadets as the training year was about to begin?

Danthorpe said, in a voice tinged with contempt, "What's the matter Eskow? You look worried."

"Leave him alone," I said sharply. But Bob's expression had disturbed me too. His face had been pale with the pallor of the deeps, but he looked even paler now.

Danthorpe squinted down at him. "Maybe you're afraid of—seaquakes," he said softly.

Bob straightened up abruptly, glaring at him.

I knew that Bob was under pressure. He had driven himself far too hard ever since his first moments in the Academy, oppressed by the grinding fear of washing out. I knew that our adventures in the Tonga Trench had drained his last reserves; yet I couldn't quite understand this now.

Then he relaxed and looked away. "I guess that's so," he said, barely loud enough to be heard. "I guess I'm afraid of quakes."

"Then Krakatoa Dome's no place for you! We've got plenty of them there!" Danthorpe was smirking smugly—as though he were actually boasting of the fact, as if the quakes were another valuable resource of the seabottom around Krakatoa, like the oil. "It's near the great geological fault, where the crust of the earth buckles down in the Java Trough. Ever hear of the great eruption of Krakatoa, back a hundred years and more ago? It made waves a hundred feet high—on the surface, of course. That was part of the instability of the area!"

I interrupted him, really curious. "Danthorpe, what's so good about sub-seaquakes?"

I couldn't help asking it. Earthquakes on dry land are bad enough, of course. But under the sea they can be a

4

thousand times worse. Even a minor quake can snap a transportation tube or turn the mad sea into the tunnels of a mine; even a very small one can shatter the delicate film of edenite armor for a second. And a second is all the deeps need to splinter a city dome.

Danthorpe had a cocky grin. "Good? Why, they're the best part of it, Eden! Quakes scare the lubbers away!"

He sounded really happy. "That leaves richer diggings for the man with the inside drift," he cried. "Take my Dad. He's making plenty, down in Krakatoa Dome. He isn't worried about sub-sea quakes!"

Suddenly something registered in my mind. "Your dad?" I repeated. "Danthorpe? Then your father must be—"

He nodded. "You've heard of him," he said proudly. "Sure you have! He bought in at the bottom level at Krakatoa Dome, when it wasn't anything but six edenite bubbles linked together and a hope for the future. And he's traded his way to the top! Every time there's a quake, prices go down—he buys—and he gets richer! He's got a seat on the Stock Exchange, and he's on the Dome Council. He's lived down deep so long that people call him Barnacle Ben—"

Bob was getting more and more annoyed. He interrupted: "Barnacle Ben! If you ask me, that's a good name—he sounds like a parasite! If you want to talk about *real* pioneers—the inventors and explorers who really opened up the floor of the sea when the dry land got overcrowded—you ought to ask Jim about his uncle Stewart. Stewart Eden—the man who invented Edenite!"

Danthorpe stopped short.

He squinted at me sharply. "Old Stewart Eden is your uncle?"

"That's right," I told him shortly. I don't like to boast about it—Uncle Stewart says that family is only important for the inspiration and help it gives you, not for what effect a famous relative may have on somebody else. But I won't deny that I am proud to be related to the man who made the whole sub-sea empire possible.

There was a pause.

Then, "My Dad could buy him out," Danthorpe said

challengingly, "and never miss the change." I didn't say a word, though he waited—that was part of what I had learned from my Uncle Stewart. Danthorpe squinted at Bob. "All right, Eskow," he said. "What about *your* folks?"

Bob's face hardened. "Well, what about them?"

"Haven't you got a family? Give me the inside drift. Who are they? What do they amount to? Where do they live? What does your old man do?"

"They're just—people," Bob said slowly. "My father makes a living."

"Down deep?" challenged Danthorpe. "Or is he a lubber?"

That was too much. I cut in. "Leave him alone, Danthorpe," I said. "Look. If there's any truth to this inside drift you came buzzing around with, the three of us are going to have to get along together. Let's start even! Forget about families—let's just concentrate on our job, whatever it's going to be."

Danthorpe shrugged lazily. He pointed at Bob, who was staring out at the tiny white fin of a catboat, miles out on the smiling surface of the sea. "Better get him started on concentrating," Danthorpe advised. "Because, to tell you the truth, it looks to me as though he's the wrong man for Krakatoa! It isn't a place for anybody who's afraid of quakes!"

Bob and I walked back to the barracks after Danthorpe had left. I could see that he was feeling low, and I tried to cheer him up.

"After all," I told him, "we haven't got any special orders yet. Maybe we'll start the fall term with everybody else."

He shook his head glumly. "I don't think so. What's that on the bulletin board?"

A fourth-year orderly was smoothing an order slip on the adhesive board just inside our barracks. We read over his shoulder.

It was for us, all right:

The cadets named herein will report to the Commandant's Office at 1700 hours this date:

6

Cadet Danthorpe, Harley
Cadet Eden, James
Cadet Eskow, Robert

We looked at each other.

A thought struck me.

"I wonder if— But the O.O.D. said thirteen hundred hours. Remember? When he spotted me at the deepwater pool?"

Bob shook his head. "I didn't hear him. I must've been underwater at the time."

But the orderly turned sharply, saluted, and said in a brisk tone: "Sir! Cadet Tilden, Walter S., requests permission to address an upperclassman."

It was a good example of proper form; I couldn't help admiring him—far better than I had been able to do when I first came to the Academy. I said: "Proceed, Cadet Tilden!"

Staring into space, at full attention, his chin tucked so far back into his collar that he could hardly move his jaw to speak, he said: "Sir, Cadet Eden has *two* appointments. The one at thirteen hundred hours concerns the possible death of his uncle, Stewart Eden!"

## 2

# The Man Called Father Tide

Etched in silver over the sea-coral portals of the Administration Building was the motto of the Academy:
*The Tides Don't Wait!*
But I did.

I was ten minutes early for my appointment with the Commandant; but to the Commandant, 1300 hours meant exactly that, and not a minute before or after. I sat at attention in his anteroom, and wondered, without joy, just how nearly right the orderly had been in his guess about why the Commandant wanted to see me.

My uncle Stewart Eden was my only near relative. His home was ten thousand miles away and three miles straight down, in the undersea nation of Marinia. He had been in ill health, that I knew. Perhaps his illness had grown worse, and—

No. I closed my mind to that thought. In any case, the orderly had said *"possible* death," and that didn't sound like illness.

I put aside the attempt to think and concentrated only on sitting there and waiting.

Precisely at 1300 the Commandant appeared.

He approached from the officers' mess, a towering, frowning giant of a man, powerful as the sea itself. Beside him was a neat little man in clerical black, trotting to keep up with the Commandant's great strides, talking very urgently.

8

"Ten-*hut!*" barked the cadet sentry, presenting arms. I sprang to attention.

The Commandant paused on his way into his private office, the tiny stranger behind him.

"Cadet Eden," said the Commandant gravely. "You have a visitor. This is Father Jonah Tidesley, of the Society of Jesus. He has come a long way to see you."

I remember shaking the little man's hand, but I don't remember much else except that I found myself with the Commandant and Father Tidesley, in the Commandant's private office. I remember noticing that the Commandant was full of a quiet respect for the priest; I remember him looking at me with a look that was disturbingly keen. They said that the Commandant was able to read the minds of cadets, and for a moment I thought it was true—

Then I concentrated on what Father Tidesley was saying.

"I knew your uncle, Jim," he said in a clear, warm voice. "Perhaps you've heard him speak of me. He usually called me Father Tide—everybody does."

"I don't remember, sir," I said. "But I seldom see my uncle."

He nodded cheerfully. He was an amiable little man, but his sea-blue eyes were as sharp as the Commandant's. He wasn't young. His face was round and plump, but his red cheeks were seamed like sea-coral. I couldn't guess his age—or his connection with my uncle, or what he wanted with me, for that matter.

"Sit down, Jim," he beamed, "sit down." I glanced at the Commandant, who nodded. "I've heard about your adventure with the sea serpents, Jim," he went on. "Ah, that must have been quite an adventure! I've always longed to see the Tonga Trench. But it hasn't been possible, though perhaps some day— But you've done more than that, Jim. Oh, I know a great deal about you, boy, though we've never met." He went on and on. It was true; he surprised me. Not only because he knew so much of my own life—Uncle Stewart might well have told him that—but because he knew that other world so well, that world "down deep" which is stranger to most lubbers than the mountains of the moon.

9

Lubber! It was the most foolish thought I had ever had—Father Tide a lubber! But I didn't know him well, not then.

He talked for several minutes; I believe he was trying to put me at my ease, and he succeeded. But at last he opened a briefcase.

"Jim," he said, "look at this." He took out a thick plastic envelope and spilled its contents on the desk before me.

"Do you recognize these articles?" he asked me solemnly.

I reached out and touched them.

But it was hardly necessary.

There was a worn silver ring, set with a milky Tonga pearl. There was a watch—a fine wrist chronometer in a plain case of stainless steel. There were coins and a few small bills—some of them American, the rest Marinian dollars. And there was a torn envelope.

I didn't have to look at the address. I knew what it would be. It was for Mr. Stewart Eden, at his office in the undersea city of Thetis, Marinia.

I recognized them at once. The address on the envelope was my own writing. The ring was my uncle's—the pearl a gift from his old friend Jason Craken. The watch was the one my father had given Uncle Stewart many a long year ago.

I said, as calmly as I could: "They are my uncle's. Stewart Eden."

Father Tide looked at me compassionately for a long, thoughtful moment.

Then he gathered up the articles and began to replace them in the plastic wrapper. "I was afraid they were," he said softly.

"Has something happened to Uncle Stewart?" I demanded.

"I don't know, Jim. I was hoping you could tell me."

"Tell you? But how could I? Where did you get these things?"

Father Tide replaced the plastic envelope in his briefcase and looked at me across the desk.

"I found them in a sea-car," he said softly. "Bear with me, Jim. Let me explain this my own way."

10

He got up and began to pace restlessly around the room.

"Perhaps you know," he said in that warm, clear voice, "that our order has pioneered in vulcanology and seismology—that is, in the scientific study of volcanoes and earthquakes. I myself am something of a specialist in the undersea phenomena associated with these things."

I nodded uneasily.

"Two weeks ago," he went on, pausing by the window to look out at the bright Bermudan sea, "there was a sudden eruption in the Indian Ocean. It was entirely unexpected."

That made me speak. "Unexpected? But—I mean, sir, isn't it true that these things can be forecast?"

He whirled and nodded. "Yes, Jim! It is very nearly a science these days. But this one was *not* forecast. There was nothing to indicate any activity in that area—nothing at all.

"But all the same the eruption occurred. I was at Krakatoa Dome when the waves from this disturbance were picked up by the seismographs there," he went on deliberately. "The epicenter was less than two thousand miles away. I set out at once to make observations on the spot. By the following night I was at the epicenter."

Though what he was saying told me nothing about what had happened to my uncle, it increased my respect for Father Tide. I couldn't help being interested.

He told me: "The surface of the sea was still agitated. Beneath, I found a new flow of lava and mud that had spread over dozens of square miles. The lava was still hot, and the explosions of steam were considerable, even though my own sea-car is designed for use in the vicinity of seaquakes. I don't suppose you know the area, but it is almost uninhabited. Fortunately! If there had been a city dome in the area, it would have been destroyed with enormous loss of life. Even so, I fear that there may be deaths that we shall never learn of. Miners, perhaps."

"Sir," I said, pointing at the briefcase, "those things. You didn't find them there?"

He nodded somberly. "I did. But please bear with me, Jim. I was cruising over the sea floor, near the edge of the field of hot lava. I was making scientific observations—

11

and also looking for survivors who might require my aid. My microsonar equipment had been half wrecked by the explosions, and of course the water was black with mud.

"All the same, I picked up a sonar distress signal."

"My uncle?" I demanded. "Was it his signal?"

"I don't know, Jim," he said softly. "I recognized the signal at once as being from an automatic emergency transmitter. I was able to pinpoint it, and to follow it to its source, at the very edge of the lava flow.

"There was a wrecked sea-car there, half buried under boulders and mud.

"I signaled, but there was no answer. Since there was a chance of survivors, I got into edenite armor and went aboard the wreck."

I gasped, "You did *what*? But didn't you know how dangerous it was?" I caught the Commandant's eye on me and stopped; but that told me a lot about Father Tide. Know? Of course he had known; but it hadn't stopped him.

He only said: "It was necessary. But I found no one. I believe the sea-car was struck by boulders thrown up in the eruption and disabled. The locks were open. All the scuba gear was gone."

And that marked him as a true sea-man too, for no lubber would refer to Self-Contained Underwater Breathing Apparatus by its nickname, scuba.

"So the people in the car were able to get out?" I said hopefully.

He nodded. "Yes. But I am far from certain that they got away from the volcano." He gestured at his briefcase. "I found those things in the sea-car. Then I had to leave—barely in time. I was almost trapped in another flow of volcanic mud."

I started, "What—" Then I had to gulp and start again. "What do you think happened to my uncle?"

Father Tide's blue eyes were cold and keen—surprisingly; for I would have expected them to be warm with sympathy.

"I was hoping you could tell me. Or at least—well, I was hoping that you would tell me that these things were not his property."

12

"They are. But I can't believe he was lost!"

"He'll have my prayers," Father Tide assured me. "Though perhaps he would not ask for them."

He sighed, and looked out again over the bright blue sea. "Unfortunately," he said, "being lost is not the most disturbing possibility for your uncle."

I stared at him. "What are you talking about, sir?"

"I am accustomed to dealing with death," he told me solemnly. "For that I feel well prepared. But this undersea volcano has presented me with other problems." He paused, without saying what the problems were, while his blue eyes searched my face.

He asked suddenly: "Why was your uncle in the Indian Ocean?"

"I can't say, sir. He was at home in Thetis Dome the last I knew."

"How long ago?" he rapped out.

"Why—two months, it must have been."

"And what was he doing there?"

"He was ill, Father Tide. I doubt that he was able to do much at all. He is in bad shape, and—"

"I see," Father Tide interrupted. "In other words, he was desperate. Perhaps desperate enough to do—anything."

"What are you suggesting?" I demanded.

For thirty seconds, the little priest looked at me sadly.

"This quake was not forecast," he said at last. "There is evidence that it was—artificial."

I sat staring, bewildered; he had lost me completely.

"I don't understand, sir," I admitted.

"Only a trained seismologist can evaluate the evidence," he said in his warm, clear voice, as though I were in a classroom. "I admit, also, that no point on the surface of the earth is entirely free from the danger of an unpredictable quake. Yet forecasting should give some indication. And this eruption is only one in a series of several—relatively minor, all located in uninhabited sections—which seem to follow a certain pattern.

"There have been six. They have become progressively more intense. The focus of the first was quite shallow; the

13

foci of those that came later have become progressively deeper."

"So you think—" I broke off; the idea was almost too appalling to put into words.

Father Tide nodded. "I suspect," he said clearly, "that someone is perfecting an unholy technique for creating artificial earthquakes."

I swallowed. "And my uncle—"

He nodded.

"Yes, Jim. I fear that your uncle, if he be still alive, is somehow involved."

# 3

# Fire Under the Sea

Artificial seaquakes! And my uncle Stewart Eden charged with setting them off, by this strange priest who called himself Father Tide!

It was too much for me to grasp. I was no longer worried; I was angry.

He left me there in the Commandant's office, almost without another word. I stopped him as he was going out, asked for my uncle's belongings.

He hesitated, glanced at the Commandant, then shook his head. "I'm sorry, Jim. Later they will doubtless be yours. But they are evidence. If it is necessary for the officers of the Sub-Sea Fleet to take over the private investigation I have begun, they will doubtless wish to examine them."

And he would say no more.

I suppose the Commandant dismissed me, but I don't remember it.

The next thing I remember was standing in a pay-phone booth, trying to reach my uncle in Thetis Dome. It took forever for the long relay lines to clear . . . and then, no answer. No answer from his home. No answer from his office. In desperation, I had him paged in the hotels and sea-car terminals—both him and his loyal aide, Gideon Park. But there was no answer.

This much was true of what Father Tide had said: My uncle had disappeared from sight.

I stood staring into space. I had no idea where I was.

By and by the object I was looking at began to make sense to me. It was a huge map of the world on the Mercator Projection; the map that, as a first-year lubber at the Academy, I had tirelessly memorized for the glory and grandeur that it spelled out. It was a strange map, at least for dry-siders—for the continents themselves were featureless black, showing only the rivers and a few of the largest cities.

But the oceans!

They sparkled in brilliant luminous colors. Shades of blue and green to indicate the depths of the sea bottom. Wash overlays of crimson and orange to show the submarine mountain peaks and ranges. Brilliant gold for the cities; lines of webbed silver that showed the pipelines and vacuum tubeways that linked them; shaded tracing that showed the vast mineral deposits that lay on the ocean's bottom. There was incalculable wealth there! Enough to make a million millionaires! But dishonest men were wrecking what had so laboriously been built by the pioneers of the deeps, such as my uncle and my father.

And yet, my uncle was one of those dishonest men, according to the man who called himself Father Tide.

I came to with a start, shook myself and turned away from the great map of the deeps.

I was in Dixon Hall, the Academy's exciting museum, where all the history of the sub-sea service was on display. I had no recollection of how I got there.

And someone was calling my name.

I said: "Oh. Hello. I—I didn't see you come in."

It was Bob, with Harley Danthorpe. "You didn't see anything at all," Danthorpe rasped. "Can't you find a better place to daydream than a dump like this? We've been looking all over for you."

I expected something from Bob at that point, for he was nearly as devoted to Dixon Hall and the living history it contained as I.

But he was paying no attention. "Look!" he said, pointing.

It was a tapered metal tube, four inches thick and about three feet long, mounted in a glass display case.

The polished walls of it were glowing like edenite—the

fantastic armor that my uncle invented, the pressure film that turns the deadly pressure of the water back on itself, making it possible for men to plumb the deeps.

But it was not edenite, or not of any sort that I had ever seen. For the glow of this was not the even shimmering green of submarine edenite armor. It was filled with little sparking points of colored fire that came and went like Christmas lights seen through the waving branches of a tree.

It's a model mole!" cried Bob. "Look at the sign!" He pointed to the card in the case:

Working Model of
Mechanical Ortholytic Excavator

Experimental craft of this type, now under test by the Sub-Sea Fleet, offer the promise of new opportunities to Academy graduates. With it explorations may be made at first hand of the strata beneath the sea bottom.

"Beneath the sea bottom," I read aloud, wonderingly. "Do they mean actually underground?"

Harley Danthorpe twanged: "If you want the inside drift on the mole, just ask me." He came up behind us, squinting at the shining model. "My dad has money in the basic patents," he bragged. "On the ortholytic drill. Get it? Mechanical—Ortho—Lytic—Excavator. M-O-L-E." He patted the case reassuringly. "Dad says it will slice through basalt rock like a bullet through butter. He says a time is coming when self-contained drilling machines will cruise through the rocks under the floor of the sea like submarines under the surface of the water. And he says the mole is going to earn millions for the man with the inside drift."

"Great," said Bob, disgusted. "A thing like this, and all you can think of is how to make money out of it!"

"What's wrong with money?" Danthorpe demanded hotly. "After all, if it wasn't—"

"Wait a minute," I interrupted. "I remember hearing about this thing. They're having trouble with it, right? The model is fine, but the big machines have bugs."

Danthorpe confessed, "Well, all atomic drills generate a

17

lot of heat—and the ortholytic drill cuts faster, but it makes more heat. And the earth's crust is already plenty hot, when you get a few miles down. They've got a terrific refrigeration problem."

"At the least," Bob agreed. "But they'll lick it! And— Wow!"

He stopped and pointed at the big clock on the wall, under the sign that read; *The Tides Don't Wait.*

"Five minutes before seventeen hundred!" he cried. "Come on, we've got to get to the Commandant's office!"

We stood at ramrod attention, while the Commandant came around his big desk and inspected us with critical eyes as cold as the polar seas.

He said nothing about the scene in his office a few hours before. He didn't show by a look or a gesture that it had ever happened.

For that I was grateful.

He walked behind the desk again and sat down deliberately.

"Gentlemen," he said, his voice as hard as his sea-scarred face, "you are nearing the end of a course of training. You have reached the stage when certain selected cadets are chosen for detached duty as a part of their training. On this occasion, I want to remind you of your enormous duties, and of your peculiar opportunities."

*Opportunities!*

It was a strange way for him to put it. I didn't say anything. I didn't even move. But I could hear Bob Eskow catch his breath beside me.

The Commandant was lecturing.

"The Sub-Sea Fleet," he was saying, "was originally designed to protect American interests under the sea. That was back before all the world's weapons were placed under the direct supervision of the U.N. We looked out for American cities, American mining claims, American shipping. That is still an important part of our duties. But the Sub-Sea Fleet has a broader mission now.

"Our enemies down deep are seldom men in these days. In fact, the old institution of war was drowned in the deeps. There's room and wealth enough for everybody.

18

"But getting them takes co-operation. Edenite was an American invention—" Did I imagine it, or did he glance at me when he said that? "But the British devised the techniques of sub-sea farming. The ortholytic drill was originally a German idea. The Japanese have pioneered in sub-sea quake forecasting.

"Against the hazards of the sea, all men fight together."

He paused and looked at us.

" 'The Tides Don't Wait!' " His voice rang out with the old slogan of the Academy. "That means that the Sub-Sea Fleet doesn't live in the past. We recognize the fact of change. We are quick to make the most of new technologies.

"Gentlemen," he said in his cold voice of command, "on a basis of your unusual aptitudes, indicated by the scores you have earned on the psychological tests and confirmed by your actual achievements here at the Academy, you have been selected for a mission involving the application of such a new field of scientific development.

"You are placed on orders.

"You will be ready for departure by air at twenty-one hundred hours tonight. You will proceed via New York and Singapore to Krakatoa Dome. You will report to the commanding officer of the Fleet base there, for a special training assignment.

"Gentlemen, you are dismissed."

And we saluted, about-faced and marched out.

"I told you so," hissed Harley Danthorpe, the moment we were out of the Commandant's private office. "I had the inside drift!"

But even Danthorpe couldn't tell us what the "special training assignment" might be.

# 4

## Seaquake City

We were gaining on the sun.

It was less than an hour above the horizon as the last plane of our journey slowed the thunder of its jets, dumped its flaps and came swooping in to the crossed buoyed "runways" of the sea over Krakatoa Dome.

The plane slapped hard against the waves, small though they were—electrostatic "pacifiers" had smoothed out the highest wavecrests between the buoys that marked our landing lane. But our pilot had placed the first contact just right. We skipped once and settled. In a moment we were moored to the bright X-shaped structure that floated over the Dome, the edenite-shielded city that lay three miles beneath us.

"All right, you men! Let's get ready to debark!"

Eskow looked at me and scowled, but I shook my head. Because Danthorpe's name came ahead of ours alphabetically, it had appeared first on the orders—and he had elected to assume that that put him in charge of the detail. It graveled Bob; but, after all, one of us might as well be in charge, and at least it made sure that Danthorpe was the one who had to worry about making connections, clearing customs and so on. We stood up, picked up our gear, and filed out of the overseas jet on to the X-shaped landing platform.

Colossal floating dock! It was nearly a thousand feet along each leg—big enough for aircraft to land in an

20

emergency, when the sea was too rough for even the pacifiers. It towered two hundred feet above the water-line; the keel of its floats lay two hundred feet below; it was a small city in itself.

And yet, it was only a sort of combination front door and breathing tube for the sub-sea city itself. The platform was a snorkel, with special flexible conduits, edenite-armored, to inhale pure air and exhale what came out. Older cities had made do with air-regeneration apparatus; Krakatoa Dome pumped fresh air from the surface. We clambered past the vents that exhaled the air from fifteen thousand feet below and felt the cold damp reek of busy industry, oozing salt water and crowded humanity from far below. It was a familiar smell. All of us looked at each other.

"Hup, two!" cried Harley Danthorpe, and marched us out of the crowded terminal into the three-mile magnetic elevators. The door closed; there was a *whoosh;* and abruptly the bottom of the elevator car dropped out from under our feet. Or so it felt.

Eskow and I instinctively grabbed out for something to support ourselves. Harley Danthorpe roared with laughter. "Lubbers!" he sneered. Don't you think you ought to keep on your toes? If an elevator scares you that much, what's going to happen when there's a seaquake?"

Eskow, pale but game, snapped: "We'll see what happens. I guarantee one thing, Danthorpe. If you can stand it, Jim Eden and I can."

We stepped out of the elevator, wobbly-kneed, and at once we were in another world.

We lay three miles under the surface of the ocean! The blue sky and the sea breeze were gone; fifteen thousand feet of the Indian Ocean rolled over our heads; and the position of the sun no longer mattered.

"Hup, two!" chanted Danthorpe, and marched us from the elevator station at the crown of the dome to the exits. By slidewalk, elevator and passage he escorted us through the teeming, busy heart of Krakatoa Dome. Fleet Base lay down on dock level, at the dome's lower rim; to reach it, we had the whole depth of the dome to pass through.

Harley led us through what must have been the longest way.

We saw the great terraced levels where actual trees and grass grew—spindly and pale in the Troyon lights of the sub-sea cities, but a symbol of wealth and luxury for the rich Krakatoans who made their homes there. We peered through dense portholes out at the brightly lit sea-bottom surrounding the dome, where the pale waving stems of the sub-sea vegetation rippled in the stirrings of the current. We passed through the financial level, where frantic trading was going on in the ores and products of the sea bottom, and in stocks and securities that financed the corporations that made their business there. "See that?" barked Harley Danthorpe. "My dad's idea!"

We looked. It was the entrance to the Krakatoa Exchange—columned with massive pillars shaped like upended sub-sea ships, the tall hulls aglow with a fire that looked like edenite.

"My dad was one of the founding members," Harley informed us proudly. "He designed the Exchange."

"That's nice," said Bob, but I doubt that he meant it.

Harley paused and looked at him narrowly. "Eskow," he said, "you're looking pretty solemn. Don't you like Krakatoa?"

Bob said: "I was thinking about the landing platform up at surface level. I'd never seen anything like that in the other sub-sea cities."

Harley laughed. *"Other* cities!" he sneered. "What have *they* got? Krakatoa's the place, and don't you forget it! That platform—it cost half a billion dollars! It took three years to build. But it's a solid investment." He winked and lowered his voice. "My dad bought a piece of it. He had the inside drift, all right. He says the franchise alone is worth the whole investment, because, you see, those air conduits are the city's windpipe, and—"

"That's what I was thinking about," Bob interrupted. "Suppose they get broken?"

"What could break them?"

"A storm, perhaps."

Harley grinned like a man who'd just found a million dollars. "I can show you a section of the cables. No storm could break them. Besides, the waves can roll right

22

through the piers between the platform and the floats without doing any damage. No. Try again."

"This is seaquake territory," Bob reminded him. "There could be a tidal wave."

"You mean a *tsunami*," Harley Danthorpe corrected him smugly. "That's the right name for a seismic sea wave. Man, you're *really* a lubber! Tsunamis are dangerous along a coast, all right, where they have a chance to build up speed and power. But not out in the open ocean! We wouldn't even notice one going by, except for the readings on the instruments."

Bob shrugged. But he didn't look convinced.

"I hope you aren't scared of quakes," Harley said politely—*too* politely; it was like a sneer. "After all, even a lubber ought to get over being afraid of things like that. Just stick around, Bob. We aren't afraid of quakes in Krakatoa Dome. Why, we call it 'Seaquake City'! We built it to stand through a Force Nine quake—and they don't come that strong very often. We're riding the inside drift, and my dad has got rich on all the tin and uranium and oil that everybody else was afraid to touch."

Well, that was about all the "inside drift" I could take.

It bothered Bob even more than it did me. This Harley Danthorpe, he might be a real expert on seaquakes and life in Krakatoa Dome, but he didn't know a thing about how to get along with his fellow man. I could see Bob's face tightening in resentment.

Fortunately, that was about the end of that little discussion, because we had come to the gate of the Fleet Base.

"Halt!" rapped out a Sub-Sea Fleet guard, bright in sea-scarlet tunic, presenting arms. "Advance and identify yourselves!"

Harley Danthorpe snapped to. He marched three paces forward as though it was the drill field at the Academy. "Cadet Danthorpe, Harley!" he snapped. "With a detachment of two cadets, reporting to the commanding officer!"

The guard passed us in without another word ... but as we entered I caught the ghost of a wink from him. Evidently he'd seen cadets as raw and fresh as Harley Danthorpe before!

We reported to a smooth-faced executive officer, who looked as though he'd been out of the Academy about three hours himself. He read our orders, frowned and finally said:

"You will be quartered here on the base. Yeoman Harris will show you to your quarters. You will report for duty to Lieutenant Tsuya." He glanced at some memo on his desk. "You will find him down at Station K, at sixteen hundred hours."

"Station K?" Harley Danthorpe repeated it uneasily, and glanced at us. We shook our heads. "Uh, beg pardon, sir," he said. "Where is Station K?"

"Ten thousand feet down," barked the young ensign.

"Ten—?" Harley couldn't finish. Evidently this was one thing that the inside drift didn't cover, because he was as much at sea as we were. Ten thousand feet down? But that was bedrock!

We didn't have a chance to ask questions. The exec said irritably: "Yeoman Harris will show you the way. Anything else you need to know, you'll learn from Lieutenant Tsuya. Dis—"

He didn't get a chance to finish the word "dismissed." Harley Danthorpe gulped and took a fresh grip on the inside drift.

"Sir!" he cried anxiously. "Please, Ensign. My family lives here in the Dome. I guess you've heard of my father. Mr. Benford Danthorpe, that is—he's on the board of the Stock Exchange. May I have a pass to visit my family?"

The officer stared at him for a long second.

Then Harley gulped. "Oh," he said, and added the missing word: *"Sir."*

"Very well," said the exec. "Your request is refused."

"Refused? But—"

"That's enough!" barked the officer. "As I've told you, Lieutenant Tsuya will be your commanding officer. You may ask him about it. Still, I can inform you that the answer will be negative, Mr. Danthorpe. Cadets in training here at Krakatoa Base are not granted passes for the first two weeks."

"Two *weeks*?" Harley flinched. "But, sir! My father is the most important man in Kra—"

"Quite possibly! You, however, are a cadet!"

"Yes, sir." For the first time, Harley Danthorpe's voice lost its brassy twang.

We saluted.

But Bob Eskow said suddenly: "Sir! One question, please."

"What's that?"

"Well, sir, we've never been informed of what our duties are. Can't you tell us?"

The ensign pursed his lips. Then, abruptly, he shrugged, and at once seemed to become more human.

"I can tell you this," he said, his voice a normal speaking voice now, without the assumed military rasp he had put into it. "I envy you."

"Envy us?"

The exec nodded seriously. "Your duties," he said, "are something brand new in the history of the Fleet.

"The three of you are assigned to training in maritime seismology—the science of seaquakes. You are going to investigate not only the sea itself—but the rock beneath it as well!"

We got out of there somehow—I don't remember how.

Under the sea bottom!

It was a startling, almost a terrifying thought.

Yeoman Harris took us over and began leading us toward the section of the base where we would be quartered. I hardly noticed the wonderful sights and sounds we passed—the clangorous shops where repairs were under way, the briskly marching squadrons of Sub-Sea Fleet men, all the feel of an operational base of the Fleet.

I looked at Bob, beside me.

Ten thousand feet down into rock! Would Bob be able to take it? He had always had difficulty—it was only raw courage that had got him through the Academy so far— what would happen now? If the icy miles of the sea were deadly, with a black pressure that could crush the mind as easily as the body, the solid crust of the earth would be many times worse.

Ten thousand feet down!

It was worse than anything the sea itself might bring to bear against us, I decided. Long years of research had

25

perfected ways to hold back the deadly thrust of the sea—my uncle Stewart's edenite armor was absolutely reliable, given the current to power it and the skill to use it properly.

But the Mole was still an untried experiment!

There would be a thousand problems to solve. Problems of survival. Refrigeration—as Bob had mentioned, back in Dixon Hall, when it was only a matter of casual discussion for us. Pressure! Edenite was powerful indeed ... but could it hold up the crust of the earth? There would be a shielding problem—I remembered that the first atomic ortholytic drill had contaminated a whole Nevada mountain, so that it had to be fenced and abandoned for a hundred years, they said.

I took my mind off those worries as best I could.

Bob—I knew Bob. He could learn to take whatever might come up. I had the feeling that I was diving a little too deep, worrying about problems that might never come up.

But I didn't know. . . .

And, at that, Bob's taut, pale face was not the most disturbed of the three of us; for behind Bob and me Harley Danthorpe limped along, as though his gear had suddenly become too heavy for him. He was muttering under his breath, about the importance of his father and the indignity of being ordered ten thousand feet down.

The inside drift had failed him, and I couldn't help feeling a little sorry for him.

# 5

## Quake Forecast!

Down deep there are no natural days.

Black night has been there since the rolling oceans first were filled. Life down deep doesn't need the sun for a clock; it doesn't have a clock; there is no time. Sub-Sea Time—set by the Fleet Observatory at Bermuda—is everywhere the same.

At 15:15 hours, Yeoman Harris appeared at our quarters to escort us down to Station K.

We dropped in an elevator down to the very base of the city—below dock level, even, but not anywhere near down as far as we were to go. Here we passed through gloomy storage spaces, with glimpses of dark tunnels choked with air conduits and the coiled piping that served the city above. We could hear the bass throbbing of the pumps that sucked the trickling waste water from all the myriad drains and catch basins of the city, collected it in sumps and forced it, under fantastic pressure, out into the hungrily thrusting sea outside. We walked out into an arched tunnel whose dripping roof was black basaltic rock, still marked with the ragged bite of the drills that had cut it out of the sea's bottom when the Dome was built.

"We're halfway," said Yeoman Harris dourly. He wasn't much of a talker.

An armed guard stepped briskly out of a little sheet-metal shelter. "Halt!"

27

Yeoman Harris stepped up and showed him a copy of our orders. This was no courtesy inspection, no military drill. This was real business. The guard scanned every word and line, and when he handed the orders back to Harris I had the feeling that he had memorized them.

This was serious business—that much was for sure.

"Come on," growled the wheezing old yeoman. He led us past the guard, to yet another elevator.

But this one was something new in my experience.

It was a small round cage, and it hung in a circular shaft. But the shaft was hewn out of living rock, and it glowed with a shimmering inside film of edenite.

Here was pressure beyond anything I had experienced! Even the rigid basalt that cups the world's oceans was not to be trusted down here; it might crumble, it might flow under the mighty weight of sea and rock above, and so it must be lined with edenite!

Harris herded us into the cage and pressed a button.

The cage dropped out from under us into the palely shining bore. The walls shimmered with a thousand shades of color as we fell, reflecting the play of pressure that they contained; it was a reassuring sight to me, since edenite was something I had grown up with, a familiar story in my family. But Harley Danthorpe was chalk white.

And Bob kept his face turned away.

We came out of the cage in a matter of minutes—ten thousand feet down. Above us was nearly two miles of solid rock. Above that, the massive bulk of Krakatoa Dome, the entire city of people and industry, the fleet base and the soaring pillars of the Exchange—far, far over our heads.

And above that—three tall miles of the Indian Ocean.

We came out of the cage, through an edenite lock, into an arched tunnel.

Here there was no edenite. Perhaps it was only the narrow shaft that was vulnerable, for here was only the rough facing of pressure-concrete, and it was dark with moisture. Ten thousand feet under the nearest free water, it yet was dappled with beads of water that stood out on it everywhere, forced through it by the enormous pressure behind. They grew slowly, even as we watched; they gathered into tiny silent rivulets, and trickled down into little gutters cut into the basalt floor around the walls.

"No edenite down here," Yeoman Harris explained gruffly. "Can't have it. Couldn't get through to the rock when we go out in the Moles."

We looked at each other wordlessly. There wasn't anything to say.

White light poured down on us from isotopic Troyon tubes.

We stood in a narrow little tomb of an office, saluted, and reported to Lieutenant Tsuya, our new commanding officer.

"Danthorpe," he said cheerfully. "Eskow. Eden." He shook hands all around. He was lean and young and intense looking, and very much alive. "Glad to see you, Eden," he said, pumping my hand. "I know a lot about your uncle. Good man. Don't pay any attention to what some people say. They're just jealous."

"Thanks," I said—but it wasn't the kind of thing I liked to hear. So the gossip about Uncle Stewart had penetrated this far!

But he was going on to the others. "Good to have you aboard," he said. "Sit down. We'll get started right away."

I sat, and so did the others. It was cold there, in that room. In spite of the light, it still seemed gloomy, from the wet blackness of the walls and from the smothering darkness of miles of rock and water that all of us knew were overhead.

Cold?

Lieutenant Tsuya grinned; he said accurately: "You're wondering why it isn't hot here."

I nodded. It was odd; this far down, the Earth's internal heat should have raised the temperature a degree or two, not cut it down. No doubt the air conditioning would make it bearable—but this was definitely chilly.

"Partly psychological," said Lieutenant Tsuya, his pumpkin-shaped face smiling. "Partly because of the flow of water—we've pretty well honeycombed the rock around here. Don't worry. It'll get hot enough when you start using your geosondes."

"Geosondes—" Danthorpe swallowed. "Lieutenant," he said desperately, "I'd like to request a twenty-four hour pass at once, for the purpose of visiting my family."

"Family?"

"My Dad," said Harley Danthorpe proudly. "Mr. Benford Danthorpe. He's a very important—"

"I know," said the Lieutenant, the smile fading. "There won't be any passes, however. Not for some time.

"For the next two weeks, all three of you will be occupied sixteen hours a day. None of you is going to have any spare time at all. You will be on duty for all except eight hours in every twenty-four—and those eight will be used for sleep.

"You'll need it."

He sat down and twisted a dial on his desk. On the wall behind him there appeared a map—a strange map, such as I had never seen before. It seemed to show the contours of the sea bottom, but it was overlaid with lines and shaded areas that looked like nothing I could recognize.

"You have been assigned," said Lieutenant Tsuya, "to one of the most difficult and exacting studies that you will undertake in all your sub-sea careers. As a small part of it, you will take part in investigation of the rock around us, five miles under the surface of the sea, two miles deep into solid rock.

"Gentlemen, I can hardly exaggerate the importance of what you are going to do here."

He paused for a second.

Then he said:

"You are here for one reason only. You are going to learn the science of forecasting sub-sea quakes."

What a two week period!

The first days in the Academy were rough and rugged, but nothing like this. Without a break—almost without time to catch our breaths—we were plunged into long, sweating hours in that dismal dungeon under the rock sea floor. Study and practice and more study, with the lash of Lieutenant Tsuya's sardonic tongue stinging us on. He was a good man, that Lieutenant Tsuya; but his orders were to pump us full of the lore of sub-sea seismology in two short weeks.

He was determined to do it if it killed us. As a matter of fact, it felt as if he came pretty close!

First was theory:

Long hours of lecture, study, examination. What is the earth's crust? Rock. Is rock solid? No—not under pressure! For under pressure even rock flows. Does it flow evenly? No! It sticks and slips, and pressures build up.

"Quakes happen," droned the lieutenant, "because the rock is not completely plastic. Stresses accumulate. They grow. They build up—and then, *bang*. They are released.

"Quakes are simply the vibrations that dissipate the energy of these suddenly released stresses."

We had to learn all sorts of strange new words, the language of seaquakes. I remember Bob mumbling, "Epicenter, epicenter—if they mean the center of a quake, why don't they say it?"

And Harley Danthorpe: "Lubber! The epicenter is the point on the surface of the earth just *above* the center! Why, the center may be twenty miles down."

We had to learn the three chief types of seismic wave:

The thrusting, hammering primary "P" wave—the first to reach instruments, because it is the fastest, racing through the substrata of the earth at five miles a second. The secondary "S" wave—three miles a second, vibrating at right angles to the direction of its travel, like the shaking of a clothesline or the cracking of a whip.

And then the big one—the slow, powerful long or "L" wave, the one that does the damage. We learned how by measuring the lapse betwen "P" and "S" waves, we could forecast when the destructive "L" wave would arrive.

And we learned a lot more than that.

For one thing, I learned something about our teacher, Lieutenant Tsuya.

We plotted our first maps—like the map Lieutenant Tsuya had projected on the wall for us, showing the stresses and faults in the earth's crust for hundreds of miles around, with shading to indicate thermal energy and convection flows (for, remember, even the rock flows that

31

far down!), with lines that showed microseisms, trigger forces, the whole lore of the moving rock.

Lieutenant Tsuya criticized them, and then he relaxed.

We sat there, all of us, taking a rare break, while the beads of salt dew formed on the pressure-concrete walls and drops of sweat plinked from the ceiling.

Bob Eskow said, "Lieutenant. The yeoman told us we couldn't have edenite down here because the geosonde couldn't get through. Was that right?"

Lieutenant Tsuya's almond face smiled. "No. It is a matter of forecasting."

He stood up and touched our maps. "All this information," he said softly, "comes to us through instruments. Very delicate instruments. That is why the station was located so far beneath the city. Any vibration, from traffic or the pumps, would disturb them. You must learn to walk softly here. And you must avoid dropping heavy objects."

"Yes, sir," Harley Danthorpe spoke up promptly. He nodded alertly, watching the lieutenant with his calculating squint, as if he were looking for the inside drift. "I see, sir."

"Do you?" The lieutenant looked at him thoughtfully. "Well, good. That's why we have to forego the protection of edenite, here in the station. Seismic vibrations reach us through the rock. They would be canceled out by the Eden Anomaly, do you see? If our instruments were shielded, they couldn't register."

"Yes, sir." It was Harley Danthorpe again, but his voice was not quite so brash, not quite so prompt, and I saw him squinting uneasily at the dark glittering droplets of the sea that oozed silently out of the walls.

"Our work here is highly classified," the Lieutenant said abruptly. "You must not discuss it outside of this station."

"But why, sir?" I asked.

Tsuya's pumpkin-shaped face looked suddenly worn.

"Because," he said, "there is a bad history, connected with seaquake forecasting.

"Some of the early forecasters were too confident. They made mistakes. Of course, they lacked some of our new

32

instruments, they didn't know many things we know now. But they made mistakes. They issued incorrect forecasts.

"The worst was at Nansei Shoto Dome."

The lieutenant passed his hand nervously across his pale forehead, as though he were trying to wipe out an unpleasant memory.

"I know a lot about what happened at Nansei Shoto Dome," he said, "because I was one of the survivors.

"The Dome was totally destroyed."

He sat down again, looking away from us. "I was just a boy then," said Lieutenant Tsuya. "My folks had moved down-deep from Yokohama when the dome was new. We moved there in the spring of the year, and that summer there were a good many quakes. They caused panics.

"But not everybody panicked. Unfortunately.

"My father was one who did not panic. I remember how my mother begged him to leave, but he would not. It was partly a matter of money—they had spent every *yen* they owned, in making the move. But it was also—well, call it courage. My father was not afraid.

"There was a very wise scientist there, you see.

"His name was Dr. John Koyetsu. He was a seismologist—the chief of the city's experimental forecasting station. He made a talk on the city's TV network. No, he said, do not be alarmed, there is nothing to be alarmed about. Be calm, he said, these are only minor seisms which have frightened you. There is no need to flee. There is no possibility of a dangerous quake. Look, he said, I show you my charts, and you can see that there can be no dangerous quake in Nansei Shoto Trench for at least a year!

"His charts were very convincing.

"But he was wrong."

The lieutenant shook his dark head. A grimace of pain twisted his lean cheeks.

"That was Friday morning," he said. "My mother and my father talked it over when I came home from school. They were very much reassured. But it so happened that they had made arrangements for me to go back to school on the mainland, and it was my mother's thought that this was as good a time as any. Oh, they were not afraid. But my mother took no chances.

"That night they put me on a ship for Yokohama.

"The quake struck the next afternoon. It destroyed Nansei Shoto Dome. No one survived."

Lieutenant Tsuya stood silent for a moment, his dark eyes following the thin little river of black water that silently ran down the narrow gutter under the oozing concrete wall.

Danthorpe stood squinting at him sharply, as though looking for the inside drift. Bob was watching the dark wet concrete with a blank expression.

"That's why our work is classified," the lieutenant said suddenly.

"Quake forecasting has a bad name. It prevented the evacuation of Nansei Shoto Dome, and caused many deaths—my parents among them.

"The Sub-Sea Fleet is authorized to operate this station, but not to release any forecasts to the public. I hope that ultimately we can save more people than Koyetsu's error killed. But first we must establish the accuracy of our forecasting methods.

"For the time being, then, you must not talk to anybody about our work here. That is an order."

# 6

## The Borer in the Earth

Time passed.

We learned.

And Lieutenant Tsuya came in on us one day, where all three of us were working up our convection diagrams, and said:

"You're beginning to understand." His lean pumpkin face was smiling. He went over our charts, line by line, nodding. "Very well," he said. "Now—I have something new for you."

He took a sealed tube of yellow plastic out of his briefcase.

"Observations are the key to forecasting!" he said. "And as you have seen, it is the deep-focus quakes, hundreds of miles beneath the surface, that determine what happens to our dome cities. And there it is difficult to make observations. But now—"

He opened the tube.

Inside was a heavy little machine, less than two feet long, not quite two inches in diameter. It looked very much like the model Mole we had seen at the Sub-Sea Academy, except that it was thinner and smaller.

"The geosonde!" he said proudly. "A telemeter, designed to plumb the depths of the earth, much as the radiosonde reaches into the atmosphere!"

He held it up for us to see.

"In the nose," he lectured, "an atomic ortholytic drill.

The body, a tube filmed with high-tension edenite. And inside it, the sensing elements and a sonic transmitter.

"The edenite film presented us with a difficult engineering problem, for, as you know, our instruments cannot read through edenite. We solved it—by turning off the film once a minute, for a tiny fraction of a second. Not very long, but long enough for the elements to register, without the device being crushed.

"It is with this geosonde that we can, at last, reach the deepest quake centers.

"With it—we may make sure that there will never be another catastrophe like the Nansei Shoto Dome."

He grinned at us amiably. "Oh," he said, "and one thing more. Your two-week training period is over. To-morrow you can all get a pass."

Harley Danthorpe came to life. "Great, Lieutenant!" he cried. "That's what I've been waiting for. Now my father will—"

"I know," said Lieutenant Tsuya dryly. "We've all heard about your father. I'll prepare the passes for twelve hundred hours tomorrow. In the morning, I want each of you to complete one forecast, based on current readings— the real thing. When that is done, you can take off."

He nodded approvingly at our convection diagrams. "You've come a long way," he observed. "Dismissed!"

We went back to the base, far above the deep observatory, and headed for the mess hall. Bob disappeared for a moment, and when he rejoined Danthorpe and me, he seemed a little concerned. But I didn't think much about it—then.

Harley Danthorpe spent the whole meal bragging about his father. The thought of seeing him—of coming back into his rightful environment, as he saw it, as Crown Prince of the kingdom of the sea that his father ruled— seemed to excite him.

Bob was very subdued.

After chow, Harley and I marched back to the barracks—I to make some practice readings for tomorrow's forecast, Harley to phone his father. I didn't see Bob for a while.

Then I noticed that the microseismometer I was using

seemed out of true. These are precision instruments, and even for practice readings I wanted to use one that was working properly.

I started out of our quarters—and nearly tripped over Bob. He was talking heatedly, in a low voice, to a man I had never seen before—a small, withered, almond-skinned man, perhaps a Chinese or a Malay. He was dressed like a civilian janitor.

Bob had his hand out to the man—almost as though he were handing him something.

And then he looked up and saw me.

Abruptly his manner changed. "You," he cried. "What do you think you're up to? Where's my book?"

The little janitor glanced at me, and then shrank away. "No, mister!" he squeaked. "No take book, mister!"

"What's the matter?" I asked.

Bob glowered. "This lubber's swiped my Koyetsu! Don't ask me why, but I want it back!"

"Koyetsu?" He meant Koyetsu's book, *Principles of Seismology;* it was one of our texts. "But, Bob, didn't you loan it to Harley? I'm nearly sure I saw him with it?"

"Harley?" Bob hesitated. Then he shrugged and growled: "All right, you. Get out of here!"

The little janitor lifted his hands over his head, as if afraid that Bob meant to hit him, and ran down the passage and out of sight.

I went back into the barracks—and there it was. Bob's book, in plain sight, on the shelf over Harley's bunk.

I showed it to him.

"Oh," he said. And then: "Oh, yes. I remember now." But he didn't look at me.

"Guess I'll take a little rest," he said, and his voice was still disturbed. And he flung himself on his bunk without looking at me.

It was very puzzling.

I brooded about it all the way to the spare-parts department, where the microseismometer I wanted was kept. I found it, and then it occurred to me that I would need to check over the geosonde, since Lt. Tsuya wanted us to make a schematic diagram of it. Might as well kill two birds with one stone.

The geosonde was stored in a moisture-proof box. I

37

found it and began to strip it, thinking about Bob and his odd behavior.

And then I had no time to think of Bob.

I opened the box; it was full, all right, but not with a geosonde. It contained a stack of lead weights from a gravity-reading instrument, packed with crumpled paper to keep them from rattling.

The geosonde was gone!

Lieutenant Tsuya hit the ceiling.

"Very bad business, Eden!" he stormed, when I reported the loss the next morning. "Why didn't you come to me at once?"

"Well, sir. I—" I hesitated. Why? Because I had been too concerned with Bob Eskow, in truth—but that wasn't a reason I was anxious to give, since I didn't want to discuss Bob's queer actions with the lieutenant.

"No excuse, eh?" said Lieutenant Tsuya irritably. "Of course not! Well, the three of you stay right here and work on your forecasts. I'm going to initiate an investigation right now. We can't have Fleet property stolen!"

Especially—he could have added, but didn't need to—when it relates to a classified project like quake forecasting. He left us and went to interview the station personnel.

When he came back his face was like a sunset thundercloud.

"I want to know what happened to that instrument," he told us. "I know that it was there two weeks ago, because I put it there myself."

He looked around at us. "If any of you know who took it, speak up!"

His eyes roved over our faces. "Have you seen anybody carrying anything away from the station?"

I shook my head.

And then I remembered. Bob, and the bent little janitor. Had Bob handed him something? It had looked like it.

But I wasn't sure. I said nothing.

"All right," grumbled Lieutenant Tsuya. "I'll have to report it to the Base Commandant; he'll take it from there. Now, let's see those forecasts."

Silently we filed before him and handed over our charts and synoptic diagrams, along with the detailed quake forecast we had each of us made, from our own readings and our own observations.

Lieutenant Tsuya looked at them carefully, a frown on his bland face. He had his own forecast, of course, made as a part of the station's regular program; he was matching his—the official forecast of what Krakatoa Dome could expect in the way of earth movements, large and small, in the next twenty-four hours—against ours.

And it was plain that he didn't like something he saw.

He looked up at us over his dark-rimmed glasses.

"Accurate forecasts," he reminded us, "depend on accurate observations."

He dismissed Harley Danthorpe's work and mine with a curt: "Satisfactory."

Then he turned to Bob.

"Eskow," he said, "I do not follow your computations. You have predicted a Force Two quake at twenty-one hundred hours today. Is that correct?"

"Yes, sir," said Bob stonily.

"I see. There is no such prediction in the station's official forecast, Eskow. Neither is there one in Danthorpe's or in Eden's. How do you account for that."

Bob said, without expression: "That's how I read it, sir. Focus twenty miles north-northwest of Krakatoa Dome. The thermal flow—"

"I see," rapped Lieutenant Tsuya. "Your value for the thermal flow is taken nearly fifty per cent lower than any of the others. So that the strains will not be relieved, is that it?"

"Yes, sir!"

"But I cannot agree with your reading," the lieutenant went on thoughtfully. "Therefore, I'm afraid I cannot give you a passing grade on this forecast. Sorry, Eskow. I'll have to cancel your pass."

"But, sir!" Bob looked stunned. "I mean—sir, I've been counting on a pass!"

"Disapproved, Eskow," said the lieutenant coldly. "Passes are your reward for satisfactory performance of duty. This forecast is not satisfactory." He nodded coldly. "Dismissed!"

Back at our quarters, Danthorpe and I showered and changed quickly into our sea-scarlet dress uniform, and headed for Yeoman Harris's desk to pick up our passes.

Bob had disappeared while we were in the shower. I was as well pleased; I didn't like to walk out on him. And Danthorpe—why, nothing was troubling Harley Danthorpe. He was bubbling with plans and hopes. "Come on, Eden," he coaxed. "Come with me. Have dinner with my father. He'll show you what sub-sea cooking can be like! He's got a chef that— Come on, Eden!"

Yeoman Harris looked up at him sourly. But the phone rang before he could speak.

"Yes, sir!" he wheezed, and then waited. "Right, sir!" He hung up.

"You two," he said, clearing his throat asthmatically. "Do you know where Cadet Eskow is?"

"In the barracks, I guess," said Harley Danthorpe. "Come on, Harris. Let's have our passes."

"Wait a minute," the yeoman grumbled. "That was Lieutenant Tsuya. He wants Eskow to report to Station K at twenty hundred hours for special duty. And he isn't in the barracks."

Harley and I looked at each other. Not in the barracks? But he *had* to be in the barracks.

Harley said, "I wonder what the special duty is."

I nodded. We both knew what the special duty was—it wasn't hard to figure out. Twenty hundred hours. An hour before the little quake that Bob had forecast. Obviously, the lieutenant was planning to have Bob on duty at the time the quake was supposed to occur—to show him that the forecast was wrong, in a way that Bob couldn't question.

But Bob wasn't around.

Yeoman Harris wheezed softly, "His pass is missing." He opened the drawer and showed us. "It was there. Then Lieutenant Tsuya canceled it, and I went to destroy it. But it was gone."

I stared at the open drawer unbelievingly. Bob was behaving oddly—I remembered his behavior with the shriveled Chinese janitor, coming so close to the disappearance of the microseismometer. But he was my friend.

I couldn't imagine anything in Krakatoa Dome that would make him go AWOL to get there.

"Better see if you can find him," wheezed Yeoman Harris. "Lieutenant Tsuya's a good officer, so long as you trim ship with him. But he won't stand for lubberly lack of discipline!"

We took our passes and, without a word, hurried back to the barracks.

Bob wasn't there.

And his dress uniform was gone.

"He's gone AWOL!" cried Harley Danthorpe. "Well, what do you know about that!"

"Blow your tanks," I said sharply. "He's a good cadet. He wouldn't do anything like that."

"Then where is he?" Harley demanded.

That stopped me.

There wasn't any answer to that.

# 7

## Life on the Lid

Harley said knowingly: "You haven't got the inside drift. Take my word for it, Bob's up in the dome right now, having himself a time."

"I don't believe it," I said, but there seemed to be every chance that Harley was right.

The guards checked our passes, and we took the elevator up to the dome itself. We walked out into Krakatoa Dome, into the throbbing of the pump rooms and the air circulators, past the locks where a sleek cargo sub-sea liner was nuzzling into the edenite pressure chamber.

I said suddenly: "Let's look for him."

Harley gloated: "Ha! So you admit—"

Then he stopped.

He looked at my face, shrugged, changed expression. And then, after a moment, he squinted at his watch. "Well," he said a little reluctantly, "I'll tell you how it is. I don't mind, but I've got a date for dinner with my folks in three hours. Are you coming along?"

I said: "Help me look for Bob."

He shrugged. "Oh, all right," he said at last. "Why not? But I'm not missing my father's chef's cooking! If we don't find him by nineteen hundred hours—that's it!"

We stepped onto a circular slidewalk, and then off it again at a radial way that was moving toward the center of the dome.

42

"Most men off duty head for the upper southeast octant," Harley said expertly. "That's the White Way, as we call it—where the shops and theaters and restaurants are. Now, you lubbers want to be careful on a slidewalk, because it'll pitch you off if you aren't braced for it. Watch the way I do it, Jim."

"I'm not exactly a lubber," I protested.

He shrugged. "Depends on your point of view," he said reasonably. "You've spent a couple weeks in a dome. I've spent my whole life here. I don't know what you are—to a lubber; but I know what you are to me."

He grinned. "Come on," he said, "I'll give you the inside drift as we go."

He led me toward another bank of elevators.

"To begin with," he lectured, "Krakatoa Dome's a perfect hemisphere, except for the tube at the top, that goes to the qoating terminal on the surface. It's two thousand feet in diameter, and a thousand feet high—not counting the drainage pumps, the warehouse districts and so on, that are actually quarried out of the sea floor. And not counting Station K."

"I see," I said, hardly listening. I was scanning every passing face, hoping to see Bob.

"Those pumps are what keep out the sea. No quake is likely really to hurt the dome itself—it would take Force Eight at the least, probably Nine or even Ten. But even a smaller quake, if it hit just wrong, might fissure the rock underneath us, where there's no edenite film. Then—boom! The sea would come pounding in!"

I glanced at him. He actually seemed to enjoy the prospect!

"Don't let it get you, Jim," he said consolingly. "I mean, it's true that we're living on the lid of an active seismic zone. What of it? It's true that if the pumps went, and the basic rock split, we couldn't keep the sea out of the dome. But there's still a chance that we might survive, you know. Oh, not down at Station K—that would go, sure. But the dome itself, up here, is divided into octants, and each one can be sealed off in a second!

"Of course," he said meditatively, "we might not have a second.

"Especially," he added, "if anything happened to the

power supply, and the automatic octant barriers didn't go on!"

I let him talk. Why not? He was trying to scare a lubber—but, no matter what he thought, I wasn't a lubber. I love the deeps too well to feel that they are an enemy!

But then we were up a dozen decks, and I said:

"That's enough, Harley. All right? I'd like to concentrate on looking for Bob."

He grinned. "Got under your skin a little, eh?" he said amiably—and wrongly. "All right. Well, we're a long way from Zero Deck. This is the shopping area; let's take a look around."

We came out onto a crowded street. It didn't look much different from any business street in a surface city—at first; until you noticed the Troyon tubes that give it light, set into the metal ceiling that hung forty feet overhead.

We poked through the crowds around the tri-D theaters and the restaurants. There were plenty of people—civilians, crewmen from the sub-sea cargo and passenger vessels, uniformed men from the Fleet. I saw several cadets in sea-red dress uniforms, but none of them was Bob.

We rode on a slidewalk along a circular street to the next radial, then hopped on a slide that took us back to the elevators.

Harley gave his watch a calculating squint. "The dome has a hundred miles of streets," he said. "With the slidewalks moving at four miles an hour, you'll be about four working days searching the city—and then Eskow will probably be inside some building when you go by. Better give it up. Come on home with me."

I said, "Let's try one more deck."

We went up to the next deck. The slidewalk took us past rows of shooting galleries and pin-ball machines and novelty shops that sold little plastic models of the dome in mailing cartons. We saw a lot of men in uniform. But none of them was Bob.

"That's all for me," Harley Danthorpe said.

I shrugged. He said persuasively: "Why not ride up to

the next deck? That's where my family lives. You might as well look there as anywhere else."

It seemed reasonable.

We went up one deck more, and out a radial street that was crowded with expensive looking restaurants. We rode the slidewalk through the safety wall, into the residential octant where Danthorpe lived.

The streets were wider there; strips of carefully manicured lawn were growing under the Troyon lights, beside the slidewalks. The apartment buildings glittered sleekly with wealth. The doors were guarded by expensive robot butlers.

"Come in," said Harley Danthorpe hospitably. "Stay for dinner. My father's chef can——"

"Thanks," I said, shaking my head. Danthorpe shrugged and left me.

I rode on around through the next safety wall.

It was a different part of the city entirely. I was in the financial district now, and it was after business hours, the streets empty tunnels of plate glass and stainless steel and granite. It wasn't a likely place to find Bob. I rode on, into the octant.

This was a livelier section by far. It was the crowded residential section where the bulk of the dome's population lived—not the lavish luxury homes of the Danthorpe family, but the clerks and factory workers, and the families of the Fleet and commercial sub-sea liner crews. It had no glitter, none at all. There were a few little shops on the deck, but the floors above were all apartments. Men in undershirts were reading newspapers on the balconies. Kids were shouting and running, noisily chasing after balls in the street; women in housecoats were calling after them.

I couldn't think of a single reason why Bob might be here, either.

I had just decided to stay on the circular slidewalk, continuing until it returned to the shopping district again, when—I saw Bob!

He was talking to a man, a wrinkled little Chinese—the man I had seen at our barracks!

I was on the point of rushing up to him, and then,

45

queerly, I stopped myself. Though I hated to admit it, it seemed that there was something going on here— something that involved my good friend Bob Eskow, in a way that I didn't like. I was no spy, no private detective to take pleasure in shadowing a man and catching him at some evil act. But here was something that I didn't understand, and I could not make myself step forward until I had a clue as to what was going on.

And they were, in truth, behaving oddly.

It was almost as though they were suspicious of being followed. They spoke briefly, then drifted apart. Bob knelt on the in-walk, fussing with his boots, looking covertly around. The little Chinese ambled a dozen yards away and fed a coin into a sea-chicle vending machine— and he, too, glanced around.

I stayed out of sight.

When they were borne nearly past the barrier wall on the moving in-walk I jumped aboard.

I followed them as closely as I dared. We headed down—down and down; toward the elevators, and then down.

I felt like a sore thumb—my sea-red dress uniform was about the worst possible disguise for a Junior Sub-Sea Ranger on an undercover assignment; I felt foolish besides. But I couldn't take time to worry about my feelings. I had to stay with them.

Already Bob was standing in line behind three noisy sub-seamen at the down chute. The little Chinese had paused on the landing to put a penny in a news machine. He was stooping over the hooded screen, standing so that he could see the whole landing simply by lifting his eyes.

The more cautiously they behaved, the more sure I was that they were up to something.

I copied their tactics. A couple of cadets from one of the training sub-sea vessels in port—the *Simon Lake,* by their insignia—were looking at a display window. The window was full of scuba gear, designed for civilian use in shallow water; they were amused by it; I joined them. If I kept my face averted, it was not likely that Bob or the Chinese would recognize me. The cadets paid no attention to me; they were too busy pointing out to one another how much flashy chrome and how little practical use the display of scuba gear had.

Using the side of a chrome electro-gill for a mirror, I saw Bob follow the noisy sub-seamen into the down chute.

The little Chinese left the news machine and sauntered into line for the next car.

I took a chance and got into the down car with him.

He was unwrapping his little packet of sea-chicle, as serious about it as a three-year-old. But just as the automatic door of the car slid shut behind me, he looked up at me for half a second.

And suddenly he was something more than a sea-worn Chinese derelict.

He was a human being.

He was no derelict, either; there was bright intelligence in the look he darted at me. I was sure he knew me, but he made no attempt to speak. And his expression—his expression was something that I shall never forget.

I had thought, in that crazy wondering time of doubt, that there might be danger here for me. And danger there was—it was in his eyes—but not for me! For the look in his eyes was that of an animal caught in a trap. He was afraid! His seamed face was haggard, haunted. He watched me with hollow eyes, then looked away—an animal, caught, waiting to be put out of its misery.

I couldn't understand.

I turned away almost as quickly as he did, and didn't meet those eyes again.

We came to the bottom of the down-chute; the car doors opened; we got out. I looked around quickly for Bob—

There was no sign of him at all.

There was only one thing to do, and that was to stay with the Chinese.

Doggedly I kept him in sight, for more than an hour.

We had a tour of the entire dome, and long before the hour was over I knew that the man was playing with me; he knew who I was, and knew that I was following him. I would learn nothing. But I kept on following, for there was nothing else to do.

It began to be close to twenty hundred hours—the time

when Bob was supposed to be back on duty at the quake station, the time when Lt. Tsuya wanted to demonstrate to him that his forecast quake would not occur. He had had plenty of time to get back since I had lost him; I could only hope that he had taken advantage of the time. But that did nothing to change the greater mystery, of why he had gone AWOL in the first place, and what his connection was with this man whom I was following.

And as the hour got closer to twenty hundred, then passed it, the man I followed began to act nervous, agitated. Several times he turned and looked back toward me; more than once he actually started in my direction. But each time he changed his mind. And it was not only me he was worried about, for he kept looking overhead, staring about him at the walls, the buildings, the people.

Something very great indeed was on his mind.

I could not imagine what it was—until a terrible moaning sound seemed to fill the dome. It came from somewhere beneath us, far down—so far that it was a distant cruel howling that made no sense.

Then the floor moved crazily under my feet, and it began to make a great deal of sense indeed.

*Seaquake!*

Bob's forecast had been right indeed! I heard screams from the people around us, saw the old Chinese turn and begin to run toward me.

Then I caught a glimpse of something big and jagged sailing down from the deck-roof toward me; I tried to leap out of its way, but I was too late, too late; it reached me; I was thrown a couple of yards away; and the lights went out for me.

# 8

## Million-Dollar Seaquake

There was a roaring in my ears, and I tried to sit up.

Someone was holding my head. I opened my eyes groggily; it was the ancient Chinese; his eyes were neither haunted nor dangerous, only sad. He looked at me; then, gently, put my head down.

By the time I managed to push myself up again he was out of sight.

A medical corpsman rushed toward me. "Here, you!" he cried. "Are you all right?"

"I—I think so," I mumbled; but he was already examining me. Overhead a great flat voice was blaring out of the emergency public-address speakers:

"This is a Quake Alert. Repeat, this is a Quake Alert! Routine precautions are now in effect. The safety walls are being energized. All slidewalks will be stopped. All safety doors will be closed at once. Do not attempt to pass the octant barriers! Repeat, do not attempt to pass the octant barriers!"

"You're all right," said the corpsman, getting up from beside me.

"That's what I tried to tell you," I said, but he didn't hear me; he was already on his way to look for other casualties. I stood up, a little wobbly, and looked around. The Troyon-tube sign of a little delicatessen had come plunging to the ground and had caught me—fortunately,

49

just by one corner. A few inches farther, and— But it was all right.

The great flat voice of the speakers was blaring:

"There is no reason for panic. Only slight damage has been reported. Only minor injuries have been reported. These safety measures are purely precautionary. Please remain indoors until the alert is lifted! Repeat, please remain indoors until the alert is lifted! The public ways must be kept clear for official use."

There was no help for it; the octant barriers were down; I was marooned where I was.

It was nearly two hours before the alert was lifted—too late for me to do very much with what time remained of my pass.

All around me the people of Krakatoa Dome were responding to the challenge of the quake. It didn't seem to scare them; it hardly seemed to interrupt their lives. Of course, such minor quakes were common here—since the dome was, after all, located in the great quake belt that runs all the way from Mexico, through the West Indies and Southern Europe, through Asia Minor, to the East Indies. And the engineers who designed Krakatoa had known that better than I; the dome had been designed to stand them.

But this quake—this one was something special.

This was the one that none of us had forecast—except Bob Eskow.

I went back to base with a great many questions on my mind.

But the station was sealed off.

It was because of the quake, of course. Lieutenant Tsuya had one of the geosondes out, and it was too dangerous to do so without activating the Edenite shields between the quake station and the rest of the base and the dome itself—especially with a quake so recent and the chance of another. It made sense; but it was no help to me.

I wanted to see Bob.

I went to sleep in spite of myself—my aching head made it difficult for me to stay awake, though I wanted to be there when Bob came back from the station.

But when I woke up, Bob's bed had been slept in, but

he was already up and gone; and Harley Danthorpe was sitting on the side of it, looking at me with a strange expression.

"Eden," he said, "I have to hand it to you."

"What are you talking about?"

He chuckled, but there was a look of respect in his eyes—yes, respect, and something else, too; something I couldn't quite trace. It was as though he were giving me his grudging admiration for something—but something that, after all, he found a little disappointing. "Talk about the inside drift," he said, shaking his head. "Boy! You and your uncle have the rest of us capsized."

I got up and dressed. "I don't know what you mean," I said, and left him to go to the mess hall.

When I got back, Bob Eskow was there ... and, queerly, Danthorpe was looking at him with exactly the same look he had given me!

I didn't want to talk in front of Danthorpe, not about the wizened Chinese, not about anything for which I was afraid Bob might not have a good explanation. I only said: "I'm glad you got back."

Bob shrugged and met my eyes calmly. "You shouldn't have worried about me, Jim."

"Worry about you! Bob, do you know what would have happened if Lieutenant Tsuya found out you were AWOL?"

"Hush!" cut in Harley Danthorpe, grinning. "You two sharks ought to watch what you say! Come on, you two. How about letting me in on it?"

I looked at him, then at Bob. But clearly Bob was as mystified by what Harley was talking about as I.

"Come on!" he coaxed again. "You, Bob! Why not tell me how you got the inside drift on the quake last night."

Bob shrugged. "I made my forecast, that's all."

"Oh, sure! And you hit it right on the nose—*that's* all! When Lieutenant Tsuya and the rest of us missed it entirely." Danthorpe squinted at him shrewdly.

Bob said stubbornly, "I didn't have any inside drift. I just read the instruments and applied the principles of seismology. I wasn't certain the quake would happen."

"But it happened all right," Danthorpe nodded. "Oh, yes! You're a real shark, Eskow!" He squinted at me.

"And Eden here is another, eh? You know—" he sat back on Bob's bunk and lowered his voice confidentially— "you know, I was talking to my dad about the quake. Of course, I couldn't discuss what we were doing here—you know that. But somehow, the—uh—subject of quake forecasting came up." He winked. "And Dad says that there would be millions in an accurate forecasting system."

"Of course!" said Bob earnestly. "But the money's the least part of it, Harley. Think of the lives! A dependable forecasting system could prevent tragedies like the one at Nansei Shoto Dome."

"Sure, sure," said Harley Danthorpe. "But the money's what I'm talking about. You know, a smart operator wouldn't have to wait for a major quake. He could make a killing in a little one—like last night's.

"In fact," he said after a moment, looking at me with that curious expression, "my dad says one trader did."

There was a pause.

Bob broke it. "What are you talking about?" he demanded.

Danthorpe grinned. "Ask him," he said, pointing to me. "Ask him about his uncle."

I was totally mystified. "My uncle—Stewart Eden, you mean? But I haven't seen him in a long time. You don't mean that Uncle Stewart's here in Krakatoa Dome, do you?"

Danthorpe shrugged. "I don't know if he is or not," he said. "But I know what my father says. Your uncle's broker was busy in the market yesterday—selling securities short. He *knew* there would be a market break today! And I guess he knew there would be a quake, to cause it."

He stared at me again, with that curious sort of respect in his eyes. "For your uncle," he said, "it was a million-dollar quake!"

It took my breath away.

I knew that my Uncle Stewart had investments in all sorts of enterprises down deep. I knew that he was sometimes wealthy, and sometimes nearly bankrupt—that was the way he lived. Long before he invented edenite he had been playing a dangerous game with the sea, matching his brain and his money—and often his life—against all its hazards. Sometimes he had won. Why, all the sub-sea domes were evidence of that! But, just as often, the unconquerable sea had beaten him.

But this—making money out of disaster! I could hardly believe it.

If nothing else, it took my mind off Bob Eskow. "Come on, Jim," Danthorpe was insisting. "Where is he? Is he in Krakatoa Dome?"

I could only tell him what I knew of the truth. "The last I heard of him, he was in Marinia. Thetis Dome, I think. I don't know where he is now."

"Sure, sure." But Harley Danthorpe seemed disappointed. "Too bad," he said. "My dad is anxious to meet him."

Bob grinned tightly. "I bet he is," he said in a voice that rasped. "I bet he'd like to be able to make a few millions out of quakes himself."

It was not a pleasant remark, but Danthorpe nodded shrewdly. "Of course. They're both working the inside drift. They ought to be working together."

I doubted that my uncle would want to work any kind of drift with old Barnacle Ben Danthorpe. But I didn't say anything—didn't have much of a chance, for that matter, for just then Yeoman Harris came into our quarters.

"Eden?" he demanded, peering around. "Where's— Oh, there you are. Eden, you're to report to Lieutenant Tsuya down at Station K—at oh eight hundred hours."

I glanced at my watch. It was almost that already.

"On the double!" he said.

I hesitated. What did the lieutenant want with me? I looked hard at the old yeoman's sea-battered face. His watery, bulging eyes didn't tell me a thing. "Can't you give me a tow?" I asked. "I'm adrift."

He snapped: "Give you a tow? You cadets are more trouble than you're worth already!" And he glared at Eskow. "You," he muttered, "I'd give a lot to know what you were up to last night, when your pass was missing?"

Bob's expression was innocent. "I thought you found the pass."

"I did! But where was it when I *couldn't* find it? You wouldn't have, for instance, taken it, used it, and then put it back?"

Bob merely looked polite; but that was answer enough for me. But I didn't have time to think about it. "On the double, Eden!" Yeoman Harris barked. "The tides don't wait!"

And I hurried off to Station K.

Lieutenant Tsuya glanced up abstractedly as I came into the station, mumbled something, and looked back at his map.

He had been there around the clock. When he found time to sleep I had no idea; his pumpkin face was sagging with weariness, but his eyes were still bright.

He was working over a cross-sectional chart, with the crumpled layers of the earth's crust carefully lined in under the Dome, stretching out and under the great downfold of the Java Trough. He painstakingly inked in a red fault line, and then looked up.

"Eden," he said, "I hear you were hurt in the quake last night."

The lieutenant didn't miss much. "Not badly, sir. Just a scratch."

"Yes." He nodded and leaned back, staring at the ceiling. "Krakatoa Dome was lucky," he said. "If it had been a major quake, like the one at Nansei Shoto——"

He shook his head and closed his eyes for a second. "You didn't forecast it, Eden," he said, reaching back to knead the weary muscles at the back of his neck. "That's no shame to you. I didn't forecast it either. But Bob Eskow did."

"Yes, sir."

Lieutenant Tsuya said suddenly: "How well do you know Cadet Eskow?"

"Why—why——" He had caught me off balance. "We've been close friends ever since we were lubbers at the Academy, sir."

"I see. And how do you think he was able to make that forecast last night?"

It was a good question. Unfortunately, I didn't have a good answer.

I should have known that the Lieutenant would ask that question; as I say, he didn't miss much.

I said: "I can't account for it, sir."

The lieutenant nodded. "But you'd like to, wouldn't you, Cadet Eden?"

"I don't know what you mean, sir!"

Lieutenant Tsuya said thoughtfully, "I have questioned him, and all I get out of him is that his forecast was based on the observations we all made together. It is true that the observations support his forecast—viewed in a certain light. It is all a matter of probabilities. I elected to consider the quake very improbable. So did you and Cadet Danthorpe. But Cadet Eskow—no. He considered it probable." He leaned forward and looked at me searchingly. "And I wonder why, Eden. And so do you."

I said nothing—but I couldn't help wondering just how much this lieutenant *did* know.

The lieutenant said earnestly. "Eden, I am going to take you into my confidence. You know the Jesuit seismologist, Father Tidesley, I believe."

"Yes, sir. I met him at the Academy."

"And do you know his theory concerning the recent quakes in this area?"

I hesitated. "Well, sir, not really."

"He believes that they are artifically caused!" said Lieutenant Tsuya grimly. "He believes that someone is touching them off—perhaps for the profit they can make in stock exchange speculation! What do you think of that?"

I said stubbornly: "I didn't know that was possible, sir."

He nodded. "Neither did I," he admitted. "But now I'm not so sure, Eden. And neither are you.

"I know of your—researches last night, Eden," he said. "I know what you were doing 'bovedecks in the Dome.

"And I know that there is some question about your own uncle."

He looked at me thoughtfully. Then he seemed to reach a decision.

"Cadet Eden," he said, "your own loyalty to the Sub-

Sea Fleet is unquestioned. I will not ask you to betray any confidences you may happen to hold. But—" he hesitated, then nodded, as if making up his mind—"if you would like to continue your, ah researches ... why, I will be glad to facilitate them in any way I can.

"Specifically," he said, "if you require another pass to do any further investigation, I will see that it is granted."

And that was all he would say.

I went back to our quarters, very much disturbed in mind.

What Lieutenant Tsuya was suggesting was too horrible to believe! Clearly, he knew about Bob Eskow's absence last night—knew even that I had been following him—and suspected, as I had come to suspect myself, that Bob's forecast of the surprise quake was by no means an accident.

It was more than I could take in at once.

I couldn't help thinking of the time when I had come on Bob in the barracks, giving something to that wizened old Chinese—just before we had discovered that the geosonde was missing!

I couldn't help thinking of what Harley Danthorpe had said about my Uncle Stewart's broker—and what Father Tide had told me, back at the Academy, concerning the wreck of the sea-car that was trapped in the eruption under the Indian Ocean.

Yet—these were the two who meant the most to me of anyone alive in the world! How could I doubt them?

Firmly I resolved to put the whole thing out of my mind. I would not accept the lieutenant's offer of a pass— I would not become a spy! Surely Bob had some explanation to make. I would wait for it. And as for my uncle— why, probably he was not within a thousand miles of Krakatoa Dome! The whole thing was a misunderstanding, at the worst.

I found Bob and Harley Danthorpe getting their gear ready for inspection, and hurried to join them. There wasn't much time.

I didn't bring up the subject of the forecast, or of my uncle; I was going to wait.

Until the moment when I opened my locker, and my uncle's picture fluttered out.

Harley Danthorpe picked it up and handed it to me, then he caught sight of the signature. "Oh," he said. "So that's him. Jim, I wish you'd change your mind and bring him around to meet Dad."

I said, "But I don't even know where he is, Harley. For all I know, he might be in the Antarctic or the Gulf of California."

"He's here," said Bob, absent-mindedly. "I thought—" Then he caught himself sharply.

*What did you say?*

Bob looked confused, as though he had spoken without thinking. "Why, uh—" he squirmed uncomfortably. "I mean, I saw him. Or anyway, I *thought* I saw him. Somebody that looked like him, at any rate. Probably that's what it was, Jim—just someone who looked like him. I, uh, didn't have time to speak to him—"

I looked at him for a moment.

Then I said, "I see," and I let it drop there.

But there was no doubt in my mind, now, that Bob was keeping something from me that concerned my uncle.

And there was no doubt in my mind, now, that—no matter what it meant—I was going to change my mind about taking that pass from Lieutenant Tsuya.

# 9

## Eden Enterprises, Unlimited

I straightened my sea-cap, made sure my uniform was properly buttoned, and entered the huge doorway between the vaulting pillars shaped like sea-cars. They stretched forty feet up to the top of the deck, sea-basalt, as impressive as the entrance to the Taj Mahal; in actuality, they were the entrance to the offices of Barnacle Ben Danthorpe.

A blonde iceberg at the reception desk inside inspected me. She showed no visible signs of thawing.

I said, "I'd like to see Mr. Ben Danthorpe." Silence. "I'm a close friend of Harley Danthorpe's." More silence. "Harley is Mr. Danthorpe's son."

Still more silence, while she looked me up and down.

Then, reluctantly, she shrugged. "One moment, sir," she said, and picked up a telephone.

I stood waiting.

I felt out of place there, but it was the only clue I had to follow.

If my uncle was really in Krakatoa Dome, he had beaten my poor skills at trying to find him. I had tried the phone directory, the business associations, the hotels. No one had ever heard of him.

So all that was left was to talk to Barnacle Ben Danthorpe. He had told his son that he had heard a rumor about Uncle Stewart; perhaps I could track the rumor down.

I saw the snow-blonde eyebrows on the girl lift slightly.

"You will?" she said, incredulous. Then she looked at me with a curiously unbelieving expression. "You may go in, Mr. Eden," she said coolly, nodding toward the office elevator. "Mr. Danthorpe is at Sub-Level A."

When I stepped out of the little elevator at the top of its track, Barnacle Ben Danthorpe was waiting for me.

He shook my hand cordially—like a salesman, in fact. "Jim Eden!" he cried. "Harley has told me a great deal about you! And your uncle—why, Stewart Eden and I—many years, my boy! Many years!" He didn't exactly say what was supposed to have been happening those many years, of course. I didn't expect him to. I knew that he and my uncle had not been exactly close friends. "Enemies" was a better word, in fact.

But still, he was the only lead I had.

He conveyed me into a big, sound-proofed office, paneled with sea-wood from salvaged wrecks. "What is it, Jim?" His squint was just like his son's. "What can I do for you?"

"You can help me find my uncle," I said bluntly.

"Ah." He squinted thoughtfully at me for a moment. "You don't know where he is?"

I told him the truth: "No, sir I've heard that he's in Krakatoa Dome. I hope you can tell me where."

He shook his head. "No, Jim, I can't do that. But perhaps—"

His voice drifted off. He stood up and began to roam around his office. "I've heard strange things about your uncle, Jim," he mused. "I knew that he was foundering, eh? Made one foolish investment too many?" He shook his head. "It never pays, Jim, never pays to put your money where your heart is. Your uncle was always a great one for backing risky ventures—because, he said, they were 'good for the people of the sea.' Foolish. I told him so, many times.

"But it looks as if he learned his lesson at last."

"I don't know what you mean, sir."

"Ah, Jim!" He grinned shrewdly. "He has the inside drift now, boy! Everybody knows it. His brokers cleaned up millions for him on the quake last night. Millions! I know—he caught me for a nice slice of it!" He made a little face, but his keen eyes never left me. "Harley told me that a friend of yours knew that quake was coming. Would that have anything to do with your uncle, Jim?"

I said stiffly: "I'm not allowed to discuss quake forecasting sir." And I almost added: "And neither is Harley."

"I see. Well, Jim, Danthorpe said, "I sympathize with that. I really do. But when you see your friend again, give him the inside drift. Tell him to come to see me." He nodded wisely. "If he can really call his shots, I'll make him as rich as Davy Jones!"

I said urgently, "Mr. Danthorpe, I really *must* find my uncle. Can you help me?"

Ben Danthorpe squinted at me sharply, as though he were wondering if he had said too much.

"Perhaps I can, Jim. At least, I know your uncle's broker."

He excused himself and picked up a telephone. It had a hush mouthpiece; I could hear only a faint whisper. After a moment he put it down and frowned at me.

"I've got your uncle's broker's address," he said. Queerly, something had cooled his voice. He wasn't quite as friendly. It's down on Deck Four Plus, Radial Seven, Number Eighty-Eight. And if you'll excuse me now, I had better get back to business."

And he hurried me out the door.

When I got down to Deck Four Plus I soon guessed why he had rushed me out so coolly.

Deck Four Plus was on the borderline between the financial district and the commercial sub-sea vessel docks. Most of the buildings were warehouses and shipping offices.

For a broker's office, it was definitely not impressive.

But it meant something more than that to me. There were no pedestrian slidewalks, and the streets were crowded with rumbling cargo haulers. The air was rich with the fragrance of sea-coffee beans and the sour reek of sea-copra and the musty sharpness of baled sea-flax. Perhaps it didn't smell like high finance, but it was all a rare perfume for me.

It was the odor of the sea.

Dodging the trucks, I walked to Number 88.

It was a door between two warehouses, with a dark flight of stairs leading up inside. I climbed into a long empty corridor in the loft above the warehouses, which had been partitioned into office space. The only person I saw was a man in paint-spattered overalls, lettering a sign on the metal door at the end of the corridor.

The sign read:

### EDEN ENTERPRISES, UNLIMITED

I hurried down the dim hall toward him. Every door had a sign like it—signs that announced dubious and enigmatic enterprises: *A. Yelverton, Consulting Benthologist and Siminski Submarine Engineering*, next to *The Sunda Salvage Company* and *Hong Lee, Oriental Importer*. None of them looked very prosperous.

But I didn't care about that. Eagerly I spoke to the back of the painter's head. "Excuse me. Is Mr. Eden here?"

The painter turned around, fast, almost upsetting a paint can.

"Jim," he cried. "Jim, it's good to see you!"

It was Gideon Park!

"Gideon!" I shouted and grabbed his hand. Gideon Park—my uncle's faithful friend and associate—the man who had saved my life back in Marinia—the man who had been with us in our great adventures under the sea!

He grinned at me out of his jet-black face, smudged with sea-green from the paint can. "Jim, boy," he whooped. "I thought you were back at Bermuda!" He pulled his hand away from mine, looked at it and grinned again. "Here you are, Jim," he said, offering me a rag while he scrubbed at the smears of paint on his own hands with another. "I'm afraid I'm not a very neat painter!"

"That doesn't matter, Gideon," I said. "But what are you doing here? Why—it isn't two months since the two of us were down in the Tonga Trench, fighting those giant saurians! I thought you were back in Marinia."

"Looks like we were both wrong," he observed. "But

come in, Jim. Come in! It's not much of an office, but we might as well use it!"

"All right, Gideon. But first—what about my uncle?"

He stopped and looked at me gravely. "I thought you'd ask me that, Jim," he said after a moment, in his warm, chuckling voice. "He's not too well. I guess you know that. But he isn't capsized yet! You can't sink Stewart Eden, no, no matter who tries!"

I hesitated, then said, remembering Father Tide: "Gideon, I heard something about my uncle's sea-car being wrecked—out under the Indian Ocean, a few weeks ago. Was it true?"

The question made him look very grave.

He turned away from me, fussing with his brushes and cans of paint. Then he nodded toward the office door.

"Come inside, Jim," he said heavily. "Tell me what you know about that."

The offices of Eden Enterprises, Unlimited, consisted of two small bare rooms.

They had been freshly painted, in the same sea-green that was smudged on Gideon's black face; but the paint was the only thing about them that was fresh. The furniture was a ramshackle desk and a couple of broken chairs—left by the previous tenants, I guessed, not worth the trouble to haul away. There was only one new item: a heavy steel safe. And on it the name of the firm, Eden Enterprises, Unlimited, had been painted by a hand more professional than Gideon's.

Jim sat down and gestured me to the other chair; he listened while I told him about Father Tide's visit.

He said at last: "It's true that we had a little accident. But we didn't want the world to know about it. Your uncle minds his own business."

He leaned forward and scrubbed at a spot of paint on the floor.

"Naturally Father Tide found out about it!" he said abruptly, grinning with obvious admiration. "That man, Jim, he's always there! Whenever there's trouble, you'll find Father Tide—armored in his faith, and in the very best edenite."

Then he turned grave again. "But he worries me sometimes, Jim. You say he told you that someone had been causing artificial seaquakes?"

I nodded.

"And he thought that that someone might be your uncle?"

"That's right, Gideon."

He shook his head slowly.

"But it can't be true, Gideon!" I burst out. "Uncle Stewart simply isn't capable of that sort of thing!"

"Of course not, Jim! But still——"

He got up and began pacing around.

"Jim," he said, "your uncle isn't well. We were caught in that quake, all right, back in the Indian Ocean. The sea-car was damaged too badly to fix. We abandoned it. But we spent sixty hours in our survival gear, Jim, before a sub-sea freighter picked up our sonar distress signals. Sixty hours! Even a boy like yourself would take a little time to get over something like that—and your uncle isn't a boy any more. He hadn't really recovered.

"But he's here, in Krakatoa Dome. I left him resting this morning, back at our hotel."

"I want to see him, Gideon!"

"Of course you do, Jim," he said warmly. "And you shall. But wait until he comes in."

He sat down again, frowning worriedly at the freshly painted wall.

"You know your uncle," he said. "He has spent all of his long life taming the sea. I don't have to tell you that. He invented edenite—oh, that, and a hundred other things, too; he's a very great inventor, Jim. And not just a laboratory man. He has climbed the sea-mounts and explored the deeps. He has staked out mining claims on the floor of the sea, and launched floating sea-farms at the surface. And always, no matter what, he has helped others. Why, I can't count the thousands of sea-prospectors he's grubstaked! Or the men who came to him with a new invention, or a wild story they wanted to track down—thousands, Jim! There's no limit to his interest in the sea."

I couldn't help glancing at the shabby furniture.

Gideon said quickly: "Oh, I know that your uncle has been in shoal waters lately. Maybe he has been a little too generous. All I know is that he has been paying out a little more than he has been taking in—for a long time, Jim."

I said quickly: "But what about last night? Didn't you handle the stock speculations for him? And weren't there millions of dollars—"

I broke off. Gideon was looking somberly at the floor.

"Your uncle will have to answer that for himself, Jim," he said in a muffled voice.

I changed the subject.

I knew my uncle; what Gideon said was true. My uncle was always a dreamer. Sometimes the magnificent sweep of his dreams got beyond the dictates of his practical judgment.

"I suppose Uncle Stewart has made mistakes," I conceded. "I remember, Gideon, one of my instructors back at the Sub-Sea Academy. He used to say that Stewart Eden wasn't even a scientist—in spite of the fact that he invented edenite! He said that a scientist wouldn't have done it. A scientist would have known Newton's Law—that every force had to be balanced by an equal and opposite force—and wouldn't have bothered with any such crazy scheme as edenite, which doesn't seem to obey that law! I think the instructor was annoyed about the whole thing, because Uncle Stewart was fool enough to go ahead and try it. But it works."

"It works," Gideon agreed. "But your uncle has backed a lot of things that haven't worked."

"What is he backing now?"

Gideon shook his head. "You know, Jim," he said softly, "I'd tell you if I could."

He shrugged. "You know how your uncle carries on his business. He keeps his books in his head. He never wants a signed agreement when he finances a man—a handshake is enough for Stewart Eden; he says that if a man's honest, a handshake is enough. And if he isn't honest— why, all the sea-lawyers in the deeps won't be enough to make a thief turn honest! There are plenty of things your uncle doesn't tell me, Jim. Not because he's ashamed of them. But because that's the way he has always lived.

"And the things that he does tell me—why, Jim, you

know he wouldn't want me repeating them. Not even to you."

I apologized. There was no way out of it, for Gideon was right. My uncle had given Gideon his trust, and it wasn't up to me to try to make him break it.

But all the time I was thinking, and not happily.

I was thinking about the promise I had made to Lt. Tsuya—the promise that had resulted in his giving me this pass.

What it meant, in a word, was that I had promised to be a spy!

It hadn't occured to me that it would be my Uncle Stewart that I was spying on, as well as my closest friend, Bob Eskow—but there were the facts.

"Jim, boy!" boomed a voice from behind me.

I turned.

The door was opening—and in came my uncle, Stewart Eden!

# 10

## The Sea-Pulp Parcel

For a second I couldn't say anything.

The change in my uncle stunned me. His broad shoulders were bent. He had lost weight. His skin had an unhealthy yellow color. His walk was an uncertain shuffle. His blue eyes were dull, and they blinked at me as though he hardly recognized me.

"Uncle Stewart!" I cried.

He gripped my hand with a kind of desperate strength. Then he turned unsteadily to the chair behind his forsaken derelict of a desk and weakly sat down.

He blew his nose and wiped his eyes. "Is something wrong, Jim?" he demanded anxiously. "I thought you were up in Bermuda."

"I was, Uncle Stewart. We came down here to take a special training course." I left it at that; security did not allow me to say more. But I had the uneasy feeling that my uncle knew without being told. I said quickly: "How are you Uncle Stewart?"

He sat up abruptly. "I'm better than I look, boy!" he boomed. "I've been through rough water. You can see that. But that's all behind me now!"

I took a deep breath.

"So I've heard, Uncle Stewart," I said. "In fact, I hear you made a million dollars out of the seaquake last night."

Stewart Eden looked at me for a moment. His eyes were blank; I could not read what he was thinking.

Then he sighed.

"Yes, perhaps I did," he said, almost indifferently. "There was a profit, and a big one. But I'm not solvent yet, Jim."

He leaned forward suddenly in his creaking old chair. "But what's the use of talking about money, boy?" he boomed. "Let me look at you! Why, you're a man now, Jim. Almost an officer!" He chuckled fondly, inspecting the fit of my sea-red dress uniform. "Ah, Jim. Your father would be a proud man if he had lived to see you now!"

He sat back, nodding, his eyes alive again, looking almost well, almost the man he had been back in those exciting days in Marinia. "Never fear, Jim," he boomed, "you and I will both get what we want out of this world! You'll be an officer of the Sub-Sea Fleet, and I'll recover what I've lost. Both in money and in health, Jim! I've been afloat before, and I'll be afloat again."

He turned and stared thoughtfully at the big new safe lettered *Eden Enterprises, Unlimited.*

I could only guess at what was in his mind.

But the safe looked very heavy to float!

Gideon coughed gently. "Stewart," he said in his sweet, warm voice, "you haven't forgotten your appointment, have you?"

"Appointment?" My uncle sat up straight and glanced at his wrist-dial. "I had no idea it was so late. Why, Jim, I—"

He stopped, and stared at me thoughtfully. All of a sudden he looked worried and worn again. When he spoke his voice had lost some of its warmth and timber.

He said hurriedly, "Jim, I want to spend some time with you, but just now, there's a matter I must attend to. I have an—an engagement. For lunch, with someone I don't believe you know. So if you'll excuse me—"

I stood up.

"Certainly, Uncle Stewart," I said. "I'll go back to the base. I'll phone you next time I can get a pass, and we'll have dinner."

But there was an interruption, just as I was about to leave.

It was my uncle's luncheon companion, come to keep their engagement. And my uncle was wrong; I did know the man; I knew him rather well, in fact.

The man my uncle was to have lunch with—the man he appeared not to want me to meet—was Father Tide.

The neat little man with the seamed sea-coral cheeks kept up a stream of conversation all the way to the restaurant.

"You're looking well, Jim," he said in his clear, warm voice, nodding like a cheery little monk out of an old German woodcut. "Very well! It's a pleasure to have you with us, and an unexpected pleasure, eh, Stewart?" He chuckled. It had been his suggestion that I come along for lunch, not my uncle's.

I couldn't help wondering what my uncle Stewart was up to, that he wanted me kept out of so thoroughly.

But whatever it was, I wasn't destined to learn it that afternoon. Perhaps because I was there, there wasn't a word said at that luncheon that told me anything of importance. Most of the talk was about the food—all of it from the sea, all of it prepared in the wonderful Oriental ways that were a feature of life in Krakatoa Dome.

Only at the very end was there anything at all said—and that inconclusive. Father Tidesley had made a remark about his seismic research, and my uncle said: "I'm sorry, Father. I'm in no position to contribute any more to your project."

"It isn't only money that's important, Stewart," Father Tide reminded him gently. "And seismic research may yet pay off. If one knew how to predict sub-seaquakes, one might make a considerable profit. Or so I hear. Just by predicting them . . . or even, let us say, by creating them."

Scalding sea-coffee sloshed out of the cup in my uncle's hand.

He wiped at his scalded fingers with a napkin and glared across the little table at Father Tidesley.

He said reproachfully: "Your trouble, Father, is that your training puts too much emphasis on sin. It leads you to suspect the worst. It makes you a pessimist about human beings."

It was almost meant as a sort of a mild joke, but Father Tidesley considered it seriously. He said in his clear voice: "Perhaps so, Stewart—about human frailties. But at least I am optimistic about the possibilities of redemption."

He neatly finished the last of his coffee and leaned back. "All my life," he said, "ever since I began my novitiate, volcanic and seismic disturbances have fascinated me. Why? Because they appeared to me to be the direct expressions of the will of God. Even a long lifetime devoted to the study of their secular causes has not decreased that first awe.

"You must not think," he said earnestly, "that I doubt that man can intervene in this. Of course not. Nor do I think that man's intervention would be improper—you may call me a sin-hunter, Stewart, but you cannot think that. Forecasting seaquakes is precisely as proper as forecasting the weather. There is nothing wrong with it."

He glanced at me, and I felt a sudden chill. Did *everyone* in Krakatoa Dome know what Lt. Tsuya thought was a closely guarded secret?

But Father Tide was hurrying on: "There is another domain than forecasting—one in which meddling is likely to be far more dangerous. Hazardous to the lives of men, as well as to their souls. You know what I mean, Stewart. I mean that I have reason to believe that someone—I do not know that person's name, not for sure—can create seaquakes at will.

"If this power exists it must be used to save life and property. *Not*—" he cried—"*not* to enrich sinful men!"

And that was all that was said.

Well, perhaps it was enough, for there was no doubt that what Father Jonas Tidesley said had its effect on my uncle. He finished his meal in silence, glumly.

It was a collision between two strong men, and it left me shaken, I must admit. My uncle seemed quite as steadfast in his faith in himself—in his own brain and sea-skills, and even in his failing physical vigor—as Father Tide was in his religion.

I could not doubt my uncle's honesty. It was absolutely impossible to believe that he could have had anything to do with causing harm to a human being.

And yet—why hadn't he denied what Father Tide had implied?

For that matter, there was another question, on the other side of the fence, for why did Father Tide continue to associate with my uncle if he believed him capable of such an act? It was completely out of character—for both of them!

Father Tide remained cheerful to the very end. He talked about the fine flavor of the sea-steaks, and the succulence of the new sea-fruits that were our dessert; but my uncle Stewart hardly answered.

I was glad when the meal was over.

Father Tide left us, and I walked with my uncle back through the clattering, cluttered streets toward his shabby office. He was still very quiet, and he walked painfully, like an invalid.

But as we came to the entrance to Number 88 he abruptly stopped and seized my arm.

His voice was vigorous; he said: "I'm sorry, Jim! I'd hoped you could come up to the office with me, but—Well, I've got an appointment. It's very important to me; I know you'll understand."

"Yes, Uncle Stewart," I said, and I said good-by to him right there on the street.

For I did understand.

There was a man who had peeped out of the shabby entrance to Number 88 just as we approached it.

It was that man whom my uncle had seen a split second before he stopped me and suddenly "remembered" his appointment.

And I knew that man. I had seen him before. I had seen him, in fact, under circumstances very like the present ones.

The man was the withered old Chinese I had seen with Bob Eskow, in the barracks and again wandering the radials of Krakatoa Dome. And he was holding a heavy little parcel wrapped in sea-pulp.

I couldn't help thinking that it was just about the right size to be the missing model of the ortholytic sonde.

I found myself back at the Base, hardly knowing how I had got there.

Bob Eskow and Harley Danthorpe looked at me queerly, enviously on the part of Harley Danthorpe—and with an emotion that I could hardly recognize from Bob, an emotion that seemed almost like fear.

"Lucky lubber!" exclaimed Harley. "What've you got on Lieutenant Tsuya, anyway? That's the second pass!"

But Bob only said quietly: "The Lieutenant wants you to report to him at Station K."

I hurried down the remaining few levels gratefully—for I did not want to stay and talk to Bob Eskow just then.

I found Lt. Tsuya busy at his desk in the damp, dead silence of the station, inking in the isobars and isogeotherms and isogals on a deep-level plutonic chart.

"Well, Eden?" Fatigue and strain showed in his voice. "Do you have anything to report?"

I hesitated only a second. "Nothing, sir!" For it was true that I had no *facts* . . . and whatever my uncle might be doing, I was not going to go to this lieutenant with mere suspicions.

Lt. Tsuya hesitated, his pumpkin face worried. "It is," he said, "about what I expected."

Absently he picked up a red pencil and mechanically began to shade in the zone of stress he had outlined on his plutonic chart. I noticed that the potential fracture-plane was almost directly beneath the site of Krakatoa Dome.

He looked up at me, blinking his swollen eyes. "I've given Cadet Eskow a pass," he said abruptly. "He requested it, and I decided he should have it."

It caught me off balance. "But I just saw him in the barracks," I protested.

"That's right. I held it up in Yeoman Harris's office until you got back, Eden, because I want you to follow him."

"Follow him?" I blazed. "But I can't do that! He's my best friend. Why, I wouldn't—"

"At ease, Eden! the lieutenant barked. I stiffened and was quiet. More gently, he said: "I know he is your friend. That is the very reason why I want *you* to be the one to investigate. Do you know what the alternative is?"

"Why—why, no, sir. I mean, I haven't given it much thought."

"The alternative," said Lt. Tsuya quietly, "is to turn the whole matter over to the Security Division of the Sub-Sea Fleet."

He paused.

"Once I do that," he reminded me, "the whole thing is out of my hands. If Cadet Eskow is guilty of a severe breach of regulations, of course, that is the place for it! For I can't condone disobedience of orders, when the orders are as important as they are in this case.

"But if Cadet Eskow is guilty only of—shall we say—some error in judgment, then to turn the matter over to Security might be to do him a grave injustice.

"It's up to you, Eden."

The lieutenant looked at me silently, waiting for me to answer.

"I don't see that I have any choice, sir," I said at last.

He nodded heavily.

"Neither do I," he said in a voice crushed as flat as the sea-bottoms outside the Dome.

# 11

# The Ship in the Pit

An hour later I was back in the civilian areas of Krakatoa Dome—and so was Bob Eskow.

And Bob was not alone.

It had been childishly easy to follow him. I had waited outside the main gate of the Base, partly concealed and wearing a weather-cloak to conceal my uniform. But no concealment was needed. Bob came out like a missile from a torp tube, headed straight for the up-chutes. I followed . . . and saw him meet someone. The someone was that same old Chinese.

There was no doubt now; for the Chinese no longer carried the parcel he had seen. Somewhere he had disposed of it. And I could think of only one place . . . my uncle's safe.

The deck where they met was Minus One, just above the main gate of the Fleet Base. Then they went down again—to base level and below—way down to the Drainage Deck.

They were just walking off the landing when I followed a handful of drainage detail pump-monkeys out of the elevator.

We came to a cross-tunnel marked with a bright-lettered sign: *Booster Station Four*. I could feel the powerful pumps that sucked at the drainage from Krakatoa Dome, forcing it out against the mighty pressure from three miles of water overhead; but I had no time to think about that, for Bob and the old man were walking on.

I waited a moment to let them get farther ahead, and followed again.

This was a service tunnel. Its floor was level, with little drainage gutters along the walls. It was lined with concrete, lighted with sparse and widely spaced Troyon tubes. Except for a trickle of sluggish water in the gutters, it was fairly dry.

Abruptly Bob and the other man disappeared ahead of me.

I halted for an uneasy second, then went on more slowly ... until I saw that they had entered a drainage sump.

Then I paused for more than one second, I confess.

For that made me realize what I had previously been overlooking. I was no longer under the dome. I was out past it—out beneath the floor of the sea itself. Above me was a few hundred feet of quake-fractured rock—

And above that, nothing but three straight vertical miles of salt water.

The drainage tunnels were not reinforced or sealed, except at a few necessary points. They were noisy with the drip and splash and murmur of the invading sea; they were chilled close to the freezing-point temperature of the deeps; hardly half ventilated, they had a damp salt reek.

But there I was—and my quarry getting farther out of sight every second.

There was a three-foot drop at the end of the service tunnel, into the outer drainage ring. It curved away on either side; it had been driven by automatic excavators, and its black rock walls still showed the tooth-marks of multiple drills.

They were oozing and showering water, and the floor of the tunnel was covered in water inches deep, running sleek and black beneath the pale gleam of a distant Troyon light.

I almost turned back then.

But I had to know where they had gone. I listened. But all I could hear was the echoing trickle of water sluicing out of the fissures in the walls.

A moment passed.

Then, my eyes becoming used to the deeper darkness, I began to see a wavering gleam on the black water to the right.

It was the glow of an isotopic flashlight, already almost out of view.

I decided to follow.

I scrambled as silently as I could down into the ankle-deep water. The numbing cold of it stopped me for a second; but then I got my breath and followed the flashlight, until it vanished behind a noisy sheet of water pouring out of the fractured rock.

The situation was beginning to get difficult.

I was already half drenched. My feet were numb. I was shivering with cold. And I was unarmed.

If—let us say—*if* they were waiting beyond the waterfall, what could I accomplish? I would be an easy victim.

But I couldn't believe that of Bob Eskow.

The distant Troyon tube was only a faint reflection on the wet black curve of the tunnel wall. I peered into the darkness, took a few splashing steps. . . .

And then I caught my breath and waded forward, plunging through the splashing curtain of icy brine.

The tunnel beyond was now completely dark.

The icy water was deeper, and it was running faster. I stumbled blindly ahead, through it, for perhaps fifty yards.

Then I saw a faint glitter ahead.

I stopped and waited, but it didn't move. In a moment I saw that it was light shining on wet rock. The light came out of one of the radial tubes that sloped down from the circular tunnel, like the spokes of a deeply dished wheel, to carry the seepage to the pumps.

And far down the radial I saw two figures—Bob Eskow and the Oriental.

The radial was a straight line. I could see them in black silhouette against the moving glow of the isotopic flashlight.

I stepped into the radial tunnel.

It was steep—so steep that I almost fell. The water ran fast, tugging at my numbed feet. But in a moment I caught my footing. I found that the floor sloped queerly down to the walls, leaving the center barely submerged. I kept to that flooded ford as well as I could in the dark.

The two men were a long way ahead.

And suddenly they disappeared. For a moment the tunnel seemed completely dark and empty. Then I could see a faint flicker of light on a surface of black water.

I went on down the tunnel, guiding myself mostly by what little feeling was left in my wet and frozen feet. Water was rushing fast down the unseen gutters on either side of me, but now, part of the time, the center was—well, not dry; but at least not covered with flowing water, so that the footing was easier. But icy water dripped and showered on me from the rock roof overhead. I was soaked and shivering; my uniform was a sopping rag.

But at last I reached the bottom of the radial.

Its water poured into a sump, one of the cavernous tanks that had been excavated to give the city a margin of safety, in case of real trouble with the drainage pumps. This enormous chamber, more than a hundred feet across, was roofed with reinforced concrete; but the walls were black and drill-scarred basalt.

Water was spilling into it from half a dozen radial drains. The rock beneath my feet shook with the vibration of the hidden pumps that sucked the water out and forced it into the crushing deeps outside.

The pale light that showed me what few details I could make out of the flooded pit came from somewhere below the outlet of the tunnel that I had followed.

Searching for the source of it, I stepped closer to the pit. The seepage water was running fast here, foaming around my feet even when I kept on the narrow ridge between the two gutters. It was nearly strong enough to carry me over the edge; I dropped to my hands and knees to look over the brink of the pit.

And I found the source of the glowing pale light.

It was a shimmering edenite film—the armor of a long subsea ship, floating awash in the pit!

It was the most astonishing sight I ever saw in my life.

I lay there, clutching the jagged rock spillway rim, staring, hardly conscious of the icy water that ripped at me. A sea-car! And a big one at that—in this drainage sump, without a lock, without any way of getting in or out!

It was almost impossible to believe. And yet, there I saw it.

I couldn't even guess the total depth of the pit, but the surface of the dark water was a dozen feet below me; the rushing drainage water made a waterfall as it plunged into the pit. The noise drowned out sounds; and there was so little light that, nearly hidden by the lip of the radial drain, there was small danger of my being seen.

The long bright hull was just awash. A stubby conning tower projected a few feet above the water. The old Oriental was climbing down into that conning tower; someone else was just outside it, on the tiny surfacing platform. He was holding a handrail, leaning out to look down into the black water.

He waited—and, a few yards above him, I waited too—until a diver's head burst out of the water. A diver! It was almost as fantastic to find a diver in that pit as to find the ship itself. The diver was wearing a bulky thermosuit—without it, he could hardly have lived a minute in that water. The goggled helmet hid his face.

He held up his arm, holding the end of a line.

"Ready?" His voice was muffled and distorted in the helmet, making a strange rumbling echo under the dark concrete dome. "Hoist away!"

He slipped back into the water.

The man on deck hauled in the line. Evidently it was heavy, because he was soon breathing hard. He paused for a second, and glanced up, wiping his brow.

He didn't see me—but I saw him. There had been no error. I had been following the right man.

It was Bob Eskow.

Suddenly I was conscious of the numbing cold and wet again. The whole world was cold. I had hoped that, by some fantastic accident, this whole thing had been a mistake—but now there was no doubt.

I watched numbly while the diver came up again, guiding the object that Bob was hauling so painfully to the deck of the sea-car. The diver took great care of it; he got between it and the ship, fending it off.

I leaned out as far as I could, trying to see what it was.

77

The whole thing was fantastic. How could this ship be here—in a drainage sump, far beneath the city? There could be no passage to the sea—no possibility of it, for the whole ocean would be roaring and crashing in, driven by the mighty pressure of three miles of salt water.

And locks were just as impossible. Why, an edenite lock system was a fantastically complicated engineering project! It would be easier to build a new sea-car on the base of the sea itself than to construct a secret lock system.

But even without considering all those fantasies, one question remained.

*Why?*

What could be the purpose of it all? Who could find it worth his while to smuggle an edenite armored sea-car in here? Smuggle—why, that word suggested an explanation: smugglers. But that was ridiculous, too; no sooner had I thought it than I realized it could hardly be an answer; there simply was nothing that could be smuggled so valuable as to justify this order of effort.

And then I saw what was being hoisted aboard the sea-car.

My wondering speculations froze in my mind, for what Bob Eskow and the diver were so cautiously, so arduously bringing aboard had a fearfully familiar appearance.

It was a polished ball of bright gold, about six inches in diameter. And heavy—by the way they carried it, remarkably heavy for its size.

A stainless steel handling band was clamped around it, bearing a ring; the hauling line was made fast to the ring.

I knew what it was at that first glance, for at the Academy I had worked with such a device in the Thermonuclear Weapons Lab.

It was the primary reactor for a thermonuclear device.

In other words . . . it was an H-bomb fuse!

I didn't have to be told that the private use of thermonuclear weapons was a very serious affair.

What was this? Was this ship being armed for some kind of piratical voyage of looting and destruction? That was my first thought—but Bob Eskow didn't fit my idea of a pirate. Not even a thermonuclear pirate!

I almost forgot to be cold, waiting to see what might come next. Bob lowered the deadly little golden ball through a hatchway. The old Oriental, below, must have been stowing it away.

And Bob tossed the end of the line back to the diver—who went down again.

More of them!

Not just one H-bomb fuse, but several. Many! They were soon hauling another out of where they had been hidden beneath the water—then another—another. . . .

There were eight of the deadly little things.

Eight thermonuclear fuses! Each one of them capable of starting a fusion blast that could annihilate a city!

This was no mere voyage of piracy—no—this was something far more deadly and more serious.

I watched, half dazed, while the diver, his frightful chores completed, hauled himself out of the water and unzipped his bulky thermosuit.

When he slipped off his helmet, I nearly fell into the pit.

The face that looked out from under that helmet was the honest and friendly Negro face of my uncle's right-hand man, Gideon Park!

It was enough to bring a crashing finish to one of the worst days of my life; but it was not the end, there was more to come, and worse.

The job of loading was done.

While I watched, Gideon quickly folded the thermo-suit, coiled the line, stowed away the loose gear on the little surfacing platform. He said something to Bob, too low for me to hear above the rush of the water.

Then both of them climbed down the hatch.

Motors began to hum inside the little ship.

The hatchways slid shut.

The conning tower telescoped in, until the top of it was flush with the shining hull. The edenite armor film pulsed and shimmered and grew brighter—

And then abruptly I understood at least one of the queerly puzzling things.

Locks? No. There were no locks.

This ship didn't need any locks!

It wasn't a mere sub-sea ship that needed open ways to

the deeps; it was something more than that, more powerful and more ominous.

It was a MOLE!

It was a sub-sea cruiser equipped with the ortholytic drills that would permit it to burrow through the solid rock itself. Now, with the conning tower out of the way, I could see the nested spiral elements of the ortholytic drill itself.

It could mean only one thing: Someone had betrayed one of the most closely guarded secrets of the Sub-Sea Fleet.

Already it was diving. The black water washed over it. The edenite film on the hull shimmered and brightened again, responding to the pressure change.

Still it slid down, while the water dimmed and shattered its image—and then it was gone.

It had entered the rock itself.

A smothering darkness filled the drainage pit.

Shivering from shock as much as from cold, I got stiffly to my feet and stumbled up the radial drain, on the long return trip through the dripping seepage and the suffocating dark. I could feel the rock shivering under my feet—the pumps? Or the whirling spiral ortholytic drills of the MOLE?

I hurried, exhausted and worn, up the chill wet tubes, while under my feet, in a sea of solid rock, the tiny ship that carried two of my best friends embarked on what could only be an errand of treachery.

## 12

## Forecast: Trouble!

It was after 2400 hours when I got back to the base. I wanted a hot bath and a dry uniform—and more than either of those, I wanted someone to tell me that my eyes were liars, that what I had just seen wasn't true.

Instead, I called Station K.

Lieutenant Tsuya was already back on duty. He ordered me sharply to report to him at once.

When I came in he was sitting at his wide forecasting desk, scowling at a 200-kilometer seismic stress chart. He swung around on his tall stool to look at me. Framed in the Troyon tubes that lit the charts over his desk he looked pinched and grim with worry, even before I told him what I had seen.

And when I had finished, he sat silent for a long moment, staring at an isentropic analysis graph without seeing a line of it.

He said fretfully: "I wish the computer section would hurry up."

"Sir?" I was startled; he seemed absent-minded—absent-minded, when I had been telling him about the deadly events I had seen in the drainage sump!

He shook his head and seemed to remember that I was there. "Oh, yes, he said. "Eden. You were telling me about—ah—"

I said urgently, "Sir, maybe I didn't make myself clear.

They've got a MOLE! And what's more, it's loaded awash with hydrogen fusion devices."

"I see." He nodded gravely. But there was something very strange about his behavior. Either he didn't believe me, or—well, what else could it be?

He said, his voice more irritable than I had ever known it: "Eden, you come in here with the most fantastic story I have ever heard, and you expect me to pay attention to it. Ridiculous, man! There aren't six MOLEs in the world— and I guarantee you, nobody but a top-ranking seismographer is going to get his hands on one. *Nobody!* If you'd said Father Tide was involved—why, yes, there might be some chance of that. A very faint chance, Eden! But Bob Eskow? Nonsense!"

He shook his head, and then his tone changed. "Eden," he said formally, "I want you to think carefully before you answer this next question. Have you any evidence to prove what you have just told me?"

It caught me flat-footed.

I had been prepared for anything but this. If he had called out the Security section—if he had demanded that Eskow be shot on sight—if he had, even, raced out of the station, taking me with him, to investigate that sump himself ... why, any of these things might have made some sense.

But he was acting as though he both doubted what I had to say—and, in the second place, didn't much care!

I said, clutching at the first words that came into mind: "Sir, surely there's some evidence! I mean—well, look!" I pointed to my wrecked uniform. Icy sea water was still sloshing out of my shoes. He looked, and shook his head.

"You're wet, Cadet Eden," he rapped out. His sleepy eyes narrowed. "Can't you think of some better proof?"

I said hopelessly: "No, sir. Except that I don't think Bob Eskow will be back from his pass, until that machine gets back from under the sea-floor."

"And even that," he pointed out reasonably, "would be no real proof. He might be anywhere. Anywhere else would be more logical."

He took a deep breath and faced me squarely.

"Eden," he said grimly, "I have to tell you that I hardly believe what you have just said. I cannot help but wonder if it is entirely truthful—whether or not mistaken—or if it might be something you have cooked up to shield your uncle."

The accusation took my breath away. "Sir—"

He cut in: "If I am wrong, you will ultimately receive my apologies," he said. "But for the present— One moment!"

There was a flashing red light and the tinkle of a bell. Lt. Tsuya, forgetting me entirely, dove for the message hopper, where the alarm had signified the receipt of an incoming message.

I saw the capsule as, feverishly, Lt. Tsuya grabbed it and wrenched it open.

It bore the imprint: *Computer Section.*

And then I began to understand Lt. Tsuya's behavior. First he sent me on an errand—then, when I had undertaken it and came back with important information to report, he ignored me, challenged my word, seemed, in short, to have lost his mind!

But he hadn't lost his mind at all.

It was something else entirely. Something had happened—something so great that he simply could not spare the time to think about Bob Eskow or the missing geosonde, much less what must have seemed like a fantastic story of MOLEs in the drainage sumps and contraband nuclear explosives.

*Computer Section.*

Those two words told me a lot!

The science of quake forecasting, you see, involves so many factors, each of which has to be evaluated for importance before it can be used at all, that computers are nearly helpless in it.

A computer can do an enormously complex mathematical job in a tiny fraction of the time it would take a man, yes. But computers have no judgment, and they have no knowledge beyond what is put into them. They don't have, in other words, "know-how." A computer can solve every problem a man can, but the man has to think it out first. Preparing a seismic problem for a computer takes more work than solving it does. For that reason, computers are not used—except in one case.

That case is when the forecaster cannot believe his results.

Then he submits it to the computer—hoping to find a mathematical error.

But whatever it was that was on the lieutenant's mind, I could see by the sudden bone-weary slump of his shoulders that he had found no mathematical error. He dropped the half-sheet of mathematical symbols from Computer Section that summarized the results and sat, for a moment, staring into space.

I said: "Is something wrong, sir?"

He focused on me with difficulty.

"Wrong?" he mumbled. Then he smiled wryly. "Yes," he said, "you might say that. There are indications of a rapid intensification of deep-level stress."

I frowned. "But today's observations—"

*"Tonight's* observations," he cut me off, "show a considerable build-up, and proceeding at a rapidly increasing pace. Yes." He nodded. "Something's brewing, down below."

For the first time since I had come into the room, I took a quick look at the charts and soundings.

If his analysis was correct, something was brewing indeed. It showed on every chart. The intensification of forces in the twelve hours between the 0900 and 2100 hours observations was remarkable.

Over my shoulder Lt. Tsuya said heavily: "I'm going to order a special geosonde run. If we could get it down to the two-hundred-kilometer level—" he thrust at the chart before him with a drafting stylus—"we might have a basis for a quake forecast. But—"

He didn't have to finish. I knew our chances of getting a sounding that far down; they were very small. The pressure was simply too great. Nine sondes out of ten imploded—that is, were crushed by the pressure—at far less depths than that.

"As it is," he droned, talking more to himself than to me, "with our best deep-level data derived from the reflection and refraction of shots at the twenty-kilometer level. . . ."

His voice trailed off.

He swung around to face me. "But you see, Eden," he

said, "that I've got enough on my mind without listening to fairy tales about pirate MOLEs, without evidence to back them up."

I said urgently: "Sir, if it's a matter of evidence, surely there must be some sign in the sump itself. If we could drain it and examine the rock—"

"We'll drain no sumps tonight," he said sharply. "Now I've got to get the sonar-sonde crew on deck. You're dismissed, Eden. Get some sleep."

His tired, troubled eyes had already gone back to his charts before I left the room.

But I got very little sleep that night, in spite of his orders.

I stood under a hot shower until my numb feet ached and tingled and came back to life. Then I went to bed— and lay there for a long time in a kind of tragic, eyes-open nightmare.

Actually, I couldn't really blame Lt. Tsuya for suspecting me of inventing the story to shield my uncle in some way. It was hard enough for me to believe what I had seen myself. It was hard to understand how Bob Eskow and the old Chinese and my uncle's good friend Gideon Park had got hold of a MOLE. It was almost impossible to understand where they had obtained thermonuclear weapons. And I couldn't even guess what they would want these things for in the first place, unless— unless—

I sat bolt upright in bed.

Unless they were in some way connected with the threat of seismic disturbances that was troubling Lt. Tsuya!

For I remembered what Father Tide had said: Someone, he thought, was actually *creating* artificial quakes! *Making* them, in order to manipulate the stock market!

And then the reaction set in.

It didn't fit at all; the pattern was all wrong. It had to be a coincidence.

For there were two separate things operating here. Lt. Tsuya's charts and soundings had seemed to indicate a build-up of stress ... the rock stretching and twisting against itself, so to speak, getting ready to slip and yield—

which would be a quake—but as yet doing nothing of the sort.

Even if it were true that hydrogen weapons could cause a quake, it was flatly impossible that they could cause the sort of pattern that was worrying Lt. Tsuya. Far from it! They were much more likely to relieve such stresses than to cause them; the pattern was all wrong, as I say.

I put the idea out of my mind.

Eventually I fell asleep. . . .

And dreamed that I had discovered a crack in the city dome. I stood watching, while the seeping drops of icy water became a stream, then a roaring river, then a thundering pressure-jet a hundred yards across. I was trying to call my uncle, to repair the failing edenite armor, but the first icy spray had trapped and frozen me. I was helpless. There was nothing that I could do about it. The water was up to my chin—

Somebody grabbed me and hauled me free.

I woke up.

It was Harley Danthorpe, shaking me out of bed.

He said: "You sounded pretty desperate, Jim. You must have had squid for dinner."

But his face wasn't smiling, even as he made the old, bad joke. (It's an old sub-seaman's tale that eating squid causes nightmares—everybody knows it isn't true.) He said: "We're ordered to report to Station K in thirty minutes."

I fumbled groggily for my watch. "Wha—what time—"

"It's five hundred hours, Jim," said Harley Danthorpe.

I woke up fast. That meant they wanted us on duty nearly three hours early. And that, in turn, meant that something was up.

Or, as the lieutenant had said the night before, something was brewing down below.

When we got to the station Lt. McKerrow was on duty. He was moody and jittery. Lt. Tsuya had always begun each shift with a little talk on the forces that were always folding and remolding the plastic rock beneath the station; Lt. McKerrow didn't bother. The weary geosonde crew was making a fresh run. He set us to helping them.

Bob Eskow was not in the station. He hadn't been in our quarters either; that much, at least, of what I had told

Lt. Tsuya had been verified. But the lieutenant wasn't, apparently, very interested. He was in the little chart room attached to the station, sprawled out on a cot, sleeping, while we finished the sonar-sonde run.

It wasn't a very successful run. The terminal point, where the sonde imploded, was only seventy thousand feet below Station K.

But the brief records, when we had converted and plotted them, were disturbing enough. They showed a sharp rise in the negative gravitational anomaly. Assuming that the sensing element in the sonde had remained in proper calibration, that could mean a sudden flow of hotter and therefore less dense rock into an area under the station.

Hotter and less dense rock. For example—liquid magma.

McKerrow, looking tired and worn, studied the plotted charts.

He nodded, his eyes half closed. "About what Tsuya expected," he muttered. "That's some rise. Eden, Danthorpe. You two go ahead and analyze them. Do it separately—I want to see if you both come up with the same answers. If you've got what it takes to be quake forecasters, now's your chance to prove it."

So Harley and I got to work, side by side at our plotting desks.

I sketched in the isobars of pressure, the isogeotherms of temperature, the milligals of gravitational anomaly.

I plotted the vectors of force, computed the changes from the previous analysis and projected them into the future.

Using the geodynamic equations that had been worked out by Father Tide, I computed the stresses. I located the probable planes of fault. I measured the tidal strains, and estimated the other trigger forces.

Finally, I substituted my figures into the equations of probable time and probable force.

I didn't like the answers I got.

I looked at my answers, and then turned to look at Harley Danthorpe. Evidently his computations had led him to some similar conclusion. His face was pale; his worried squint was bitten deeper than ever; he was erasing frantically and rewriting his figures.

Forecasting quakes is not an exact science—any more than forecasting the weather is.

You understand the cause and effect of the great processes involved, all right, but a human being simply isn't equipped to see enough—to observe enough data—to have all the facts.

Complete data for a really accurate quake forecast would, I believe, require complete information about every crystal—perhaps even every molecule!—in the curst of the earth. You would need to know the temperature and the melting point, the chemical constituents and impurities, the pressure and the shearing strain, the magnetic moment and the electrostatic potential, the radioactivity, the anomaly of gravitation, the natural period of vibration ... all of those things. And then, having learned them all, you would know only a tiny fraction; for you would have to learn how all of those millions of tiny measurements were changing; whether they were going up or going down—how fast—regularly or unevenly. . . .

It is as if you were in some huge theater, with an audience of millions of people, and someone shouted, "Fire!" What is the mob going to do? There is no way to know—not for sure—unless you go to each single individual and learn everything there is to know about how he will react—for one panicked individual can throw all your computations off.

Of course, that's not possible.

And it's not possible to know everything that should be known about the elements involved in quake forecasting. You would need a computing machine the size of the earth, to store and analyze the data—even if you had the data in the first place.

So you work with what you have. The incomplete data available consists of samplings. You can't measure every bit of rock, so you take a few bits at random, hoping to get a pretty fair average picture. (Sometimes you do.) You have a few instrument readings—of only approximate accuracy, because the instruments themselves are subject to error, working as they do under enormous pressure and temperature—and then you interpret these doubtful readings, knowing that your interpretation is as important as the figures.

For it is a matter of distance; it's hard to get down where the quakes start. Hard? Say impossible, and you'll be very nearly right. Deep-focus quakes originate hundreds of miles beneath the surface. Blindly, with our sonar-sondes, we were able to probe the Earth as far as twenty miles—with luck. The rest was half-proven theory, indirect evidence and sometimes plain guesswork.

Aware of all those sources of error, I went back and did the entire computation over again.

I checked everything that could be checked. I threw out the gravity anomaly figures we had just recorded, because they seemed unreasonably high—and put them back again when a recheck of the records of the last three geosonde runs showed the same rapid increase in negative anomaly.

I substituted my revised figures into the equations of probable time and probable force, and got the same answer.

The way our equations were set up, you never got an answer that said flatly: There will not be a quake. There's a reason for that—and that reason is, simply, that a quake is always possible anywhere. The equations were based on that fact.

The best you could hope for would be a solution that would show no *measurable* quake occurring in any *foreseeable* time. Under those conditions, the solution for probable force will give the answer: Zero. And a solution for probable time will give the answer: Infinity.

But those were not the answers I got.

I looked at Harley Danthorpe, and found him squinting anxiously at me.

"Jim?" His voice was hoarse and dry. "Jim, have you finished?"

I nodded.

"What—what's your forecast?"

I took a deep breath and gave it to him straight: "Probable force: Ten, with a probable error of plus or minus two. Probable time: Thirty-six hours, with a probable error of plus or minus twenty-four."

He put his eraser down. He looked almost relieved.

"I thought maybe I had lost my ballast," he whispered. "But that's the same answer I got."

For a moment we just sat there. The dead stillness of the quake station was all around us. The walls were sweating water. Water was trickling silently along the little gutters at the edge of the floor. Over our heads were two miles of rock and three more miles of sea.

"That means it could happen in just twelve hours," Harley said. His voice had a queer, breathless hush. "And it could be as strong as Force Twelve."

He twisted around on his stool to squint at the station clock. He said, hardly audible: "Nothing can live through a Force Twelve quake."

# 13

## The Billion-Dollar Panic

We carried our forecasts to Lt. McKerrow.

"Wake up, Lieutenant Tsuya!" he ordered sharply, and, without a word, began to go over our figures. In a moment Lt. Tsuya came groggily in, and the two of them studied and checked the figures interminably.

Then Lt. Tsuya sighed and put down the forecast. He watched Lt. McKerrow, waiting.

At last Lt. McKerrow said, "It's what we figured, Tsuya."

Lt. Tsuya nodded. "I'll see what I can do upstairs," he said, and hurried out.

Lt. McKerrow turned to face us. He said sourly: "Congratulations. We've all made the same observations, and your conclusions confirm Lieutenant Tsuya's and mine. We can expect a major quake at some time within the next sixty hours."

For a few seconds nobody said anything else. The station was very still. A drop of falling water went *plink*. The silent microseismographs quivered faintly, recording the vibrations created by its impact.

Then I heard Harley Danthorpe catch his breath.

"A major quake!" he gasped. "What are we going to do about it?"

Lt. McKerrow shrugged. "Let it happen, I suppose. Do you have any other suggestions?"

Then his thin face stiffened sternly. "But one thing we

won't do," he said, "is talk about it. Do you understand that? Our work is strictly classified. You will not issue any private quake forecasts. Not to *anybody*."

I couldn't help breaking in. "But, Lieutenant! If the city is in danger, surely the city has a right to know!"

"The city has always been in danger," Lt. McKerrow reminded me acidly.

"But not like this! Why, suppose it is a Force Twelve quake—can you imagine the loss of life? Surely there should be at least some attempt at evacuation. . . ."

"That," said the lieutenant grimly, "is not up to us. That's what Lieutenant Tsuya's gone up to see about now."

He looked worriedly at our forecast sheets. "The city government co-operated with the Fleet in setting up this station," he said. "One of the conditions they made is that we cannot release forecasts without their approval. Lieutenant Tsuya phoned the mayor last night to alert him. Now he's gone up to see him, to try to get the city council called into emergency session, to approve releasing the forecast.

"But we can't just sit on the forecast!" I cried.

Lt. McKerrow scowled.

"We can't do anything else," he said.

For the next two hours we checked and rechecked every figure. They all came out the same.

Then Lt. Tsuya returned to the station.

He had shaved and put on a fresh uniform, but his lean pumpkin face looked pinched and haggard, like a pumpkin winter-killed by being left out too long in the frosts. He hurried without a word to check the instruments himself, stared for a long time at the readings on the microseismograph trace, and then came slowly back to the desk.

Lt. McKerrow was plotting a new cross-section of the forecast fault. He looked up.

"Any change?" Lt. Tsuya demanded.

"No change." McKerrow shook his head. "How are you doing with the city fathers?"

Lt. Tsuya said bitterly: "They're too busy to meet! Most of them are also business men. I suppose they feel that they can't risk the panic. There's enough panic up there now."

"Panic?" Lt. McKerrow turned to scowl at Danthorpe and me. Still looking at us, he demanded: "Has somebody talked?"

"Oh, I think not," said Lt. Tsuya thoughtfully. "No, more likely it's just a delayed result of that first quake. There was a wave of selling yesterday morning, you know. And today—well, the exchange opened just as I got up to the mayor's office. It was a madhouse. I can't even get Mr. Danthorpe on the telephone." He eyed Harley meditatively. But he shook his head. "I thought for a moment— But no. We'll have to do this thing in the proper way, through channels. And the mayor says that it will be impossible to get a quorum of the council together until after the stock exchange closes. That will be—" he squinted at his watch—"in just under three hours."

I said desperately: "Sir, can't we do something?"

"Something?"

Lt. Tsuya looked at me for a moment. His gaze had that curious questioning quality that I had observed before. There was more on his mind, I knew, than the mere danger of the quake that lay before us all, great though that danger was. And, in a way, I could see his position. For here he was, conducting an experimental, untried station, and with a staff composed of two officers—and three cadets, each one of whom, in his own way, must have presented a huge problem to the Station Commander. There was Bob Eskow—behaving very queerly, by any standards! Myself—and, from Lt. Tsuya's point of view, perhaps I was the biggest question mark of all; for it was on my testimony that all he knew of Bob's behavior rested, and certainly he had to consider the possibility that I was somehow linked with my uncle in some evil and dangerous scheme. And finally there was Harley Danthorpe, the son of one of the men on whose good will the whole existence of the station depended.

No, it was no easy position!

Lt. Tsuya said reasonably: "Suppose we took matters into our own hands, Eden, and issued a forecast. Without the full co-operation of the Krakatoa Council and its police department, can you imagine what would happen?

The panic would be incredible! There would be mob scenes such as you have never imagined!

"I doubt that that would save any lives, Eden.

"On the other hand—" and suddenly his quiet voice took on a new and harsher quality—"if it's your own skin you're worried about, then you can stop worrying. The Fleet has its own evacuation plan. And it has shipping enough to carry it out. I have communicated my forecast to the Base Commandant. The station here, of course, will be kept in operation until the last possible moment—but if you wish to ask a transfer from your present assignment so that you can be evacuated. . . ."

"Sir!" I broke in sharply. "No, sir!"

He smiled faintly.

"Then," he said, "I beg your pardon, Eden. Break out another geosonde. We'll make a new forecast."

The sonde blew up again at seventy thousand feet.

But there was no doubt of what it had to tell. Its transmissions showed that the negative gravity anomaly was still increasing under the city. Nothing had changed, not enough to matter.

When I had converted all the readings, and re-computed the equations of force and time, my answer was a force of eleven—probable error plus or minus one—and time thirty hours, probable error plus or minus twelve.

Lt. Tsuya compared my figures with his own and nodded.

"We agree again, Cadet Eden," he said formally. "The only change is that the quake will probably be a little more severe, and will probably happen a little sooner."

His voice was calm enough, but I could see white lines around his mouth. "I'm going to phone the mayor again," he said.

Harley Danthorpe came into the station as Lt. Tsuya disappeared into his private office to phone. Harley was carrying thick white mugs of coffee from the mess hall.

"Here," he said, handing me one. "Want a sandwich?" I looked at the plate he offered and shook my head. I didn't have much of an appetite just then, though the station clock told me it was a long way past lunch. "Me too," said Harley gloomily. "What's the lieutenant doing?"

"Calling the mayor."

"I wish," said Harley Danthorpe irritably, "that he'd let me talk to my father! If I gave him the inside drift he'd have that council in session in ten minutes!"

Then he looked up. Tsuya's office door was open, and the lieutenant was stepping calmly out.

"That," he said, "won't be necessary, Cadet Danthorpe. The council is in session now."

"Hurray!" whooped Harley. "I tell you, *now* you'll see some action! When my father gets— Excuse me, Lieutenant," he finished, abashed.

The lieutenant nodded. "Lt. McKerrow," he called, "I'm going topside to present the forecast to the council. I'll leave you in charge of the station." McKerrow nodded wryly. "I expect a rough session with them," Lt. Tsuya went on thoughtfully. "Some of the members are opposed to quake forecasting in any case. Now, of course, it will be worse."

Harley said eagerly: "Sir, can I come along? I mean, if I'm there, my father will know that everything's all right with the forecast. . . ."

He stopped again, in confusion.

Lt. Tsuya said dryly: "Thank you, Cadet Danthorpe. I had already planned to take you with me—and Cadet Eden as well. However, your duties will be merely to help me display the charts."

He nodded.

"I," he said, "will do the talking. Remember that!"

The city hall of Krakatoa Dome was high in the northwest upper octant, between the financial district and the platform terminal deck.

The mayor and the council members were waiting for us in a big room walled with murals depicting scenes of undersea life—a kelp farm, a sub-sea uranium mine, undersea freighters loading cargo and so on. The murals were restful and lovely.

The gathering contained in the room, on the other hand, was nothing of the kind.

It was a noisy meeting, full of conflicting voices expressing their views in loud and quarrelsome terms; judged by Fleet standards, it was conducted in a most markedly sloppy fashion. The mayor called for order a dozen times before he got any order at all, and when he called on Lt. Tsuya to speak his piece there was still a quarrelsome undertone of voices nearly drowning him out.

But the lieutenant got their full attention in his very first words—when he told them dryly, without mincing words, that the chances were all in favor of a Force Eleven quake.

"Force Eleven?" demanded the mayor, startled.

"Possibly Force Twelve," said Lt. Tsuya grimly.

Barnacle Ben Danthorpe broke in. *"Possibly,"* he sneered, *"possibly* Force Twelve. And possibly Force Eleven, right?"

"That's what I said in the first place, Mr. Danthorpe," said Lt. Tsuya.

"Or possibly Force Ten?" said Danthorpe.

"That's possible too."

"Or Force Nine, eh? Or maybe even Force Eight or Seven?"

"The chances of that, Mr. Danthorpe, are so small—"

"Small? Oh, maybe so, Lieutenant. Maybe so. But not impossible, eh?"

"Not quite impossible," admitted Lt. Tsuya. "It's all a matter of relative probabilities."

"I see." Ben Danthorpe grinned. "And on the basis of *probabilities,"* he said, "you want us to evacuate the city. Any idea of what that would cost, Lieutenant?"

Lt. Tsuya's brown eyes glowed angrily. "Money is not the only consideration, Mr. Danthorpe!"

"But it *is* a consideration. Oh, yes. It is to us, Lieutenant, because we have to make it. We don't live off the taxpayers, you see."

Tsuya fumed silently; I could see the strain lines showing on his lean pumpkin face. Danthorpe went on easily: "I don't deny that you scientists can give us a lot of useful information. After all, don't you have my own son working with you? And he's a smart boy, Lieutenant. A very smart boy!" I could feel Harley Danthorpe stiffen with pride beside me. "But he's only a boy!" barked his father suddenly, "and we can't let boys tell us how to run Krakatoa Dome! You tell us we're sitting on a seaquake fault. All right. We know that. What do you expect us to do about it?"

"We can expect a catastrophic quake within forty-eight hours," Lt. Tsuya said stubbornly. "Possibly within twelve. The city must be evacuated."

"Not 'must,' Lieutenant!" Danthorpe blazed. "You make the forecasts, that's all! We'll decide what 'must' be done. And take this as a starter—the city *cannot* be evacuated."

There was a moment of silence.

Then Lt. Tsuya took a deep, even breath. He pulled a sheaf of notes out of his portfolio and consulted them.

"I have spoken to the city engineers," he said. "Here is their report.

"According to them, the city was designed to survive a Force Nine Quake with an adequate margin of safety. They believe that, with the edenite safety walls in full operation, most of the inhabitants would survive—at least, if it were not overly prolonged in duration. But the dome will collapse under Force Ten.

"Our forecast, as you know, is for Force Eleven, possibly Force Twelve."

Ben Danthorpe listened silently.

Then, without changing expression, he nodded. "I have exactly those figures in my own briefcase, Lieutenant," he said. "Nevertheless, I repeat my statement. Krakatoa Dome cannot be evacuated. "Your Honor." He turned to the Mayor. "Your Honor, tell him why."

The mayor started slightly. He was a big, pink, perspiring man who seemed inclined to take his orders from Ben Danthorpe; he almost looked surprised at being asked to speak in this kind of a discussion.

But when he spoke, what he had to say changed things.

"My office staff has been working on the evacuation problem for many years, on a stand-by basis," he said. "This morning I asked them to bring their findings up to date.

"It is a problem, Lieutenant! And I don't think that a solution exists.

"Our total population is three-quarters of a million.

"The available sub-sea shipping could carry away no more than fifty thousand.

"We can set up an air-shuttle that would take another hundred thousand dry-side in two days—if we had two days.

"We can find emergency space for fifty thousand more up on the platform—maybe even a hundred thousand, if we stop the air-lift and stand them on the flight decks.

"But that leaves us with, at best, more than half a million. More than five hundred thousand men, women and children, Lieutenant, waiting down here to shake hands with old Father Neptune."

Lieutenant Tsuya snapped angrily: "Why don't you have a better plan? Didn't you know that this might happen some day?"

"Lieutenant!" roared the mayor, his pink face rapidly turning red. "Don't forget yourself!"

But Barnacle Ben Danthorpe cut in before the mayor's explosion could get out of hand. "That's only the physical problem, Lieutenant," he said. "There's also a psychological problem. Most of our people wouldn't leave the city even if they could. This is our home. And most of them feel, as I do, that we don't need any quake forecasters to tell us what to do."

He turned back to the mayor. "Your Honor," he said, "I move that we thank the lieutenant for his trouble, and send him back to his playthings."

There was a roar of discussion at that; and an angry fight that lasted for more than an hour—getting into questions, at the last, of what had become of funds that had been appropriated for various quake control measures.

But ultimately the motion was passed.

We were sent back to our playthings—and to the knowedge that the life expectancy of every man in Krakatoa Dome was well under two days.

# 14

## The Lead-Lined Safe

Lt. Tsuya was seething with concealed rage—not too well concealed, at that.

We marched silently out of the city hall, to the elevator landing platforms. "Sir," said Harley Danthorpe timidly, "I hope you understand my father's—"

"That'll do, Danthorpe!" barked the lieutenant. "I won't hear any excuses!"

"But I wasn't excusing him, sir," protested Harley. "He's a businessman. You have to understand that."

"I understand that he's a murderer!" roared the lieutenant.

Harley Danthorpe stopped dead. "He's my father, sir!"

Lt. Tsuya hesitated. "As you were," he growled after a moment. "Sorry, Danthorpe. This business is getting on my nerves." He glanced around him, and I knew what was going on in his mind. Here were the giant basalt pillars, the hurrying crowds of people, the elaborate, ornate offices and administration buildings of a huge and prosperous city. And yet, if our predictions were correct, in a matter of days—and not very many of them, at that—all this would be swept away. The thundering shrug of the sub-sea rock adjusting itself would topple the buildings and wrench the edenite skin off Krakatoa Dome; icy brine, steel-hard under three miles of pressure, would hammer in; in another week the benthoctopus and the giant squid would make their homes here in the wrecked, drowned ruin that had been Krakatoa Dome.

There was nothing we could do to prevent it.

And nothing the city itself *would* do to save the lives of all its people!

Suddenly—"Danthorpe!" rapped the lieutenant. Harley sprang to attention. "Danthorpe, get to a phone. Relay to the base commandant my respects, and inform him that the city council has rejected my recommendation. Suggest that he take independent action through Fleet channels."

"Aye-aye, sir!" snapped Harley Danthorpe, and departed on the double for a phone.

"Not that anything can be done through the Fleet in time," muttered the lieutenant, gazing after him. "But still, they may be in time to rescue part of the inhabitants."

I said: "Sir, if there's anything I can do—"

"There is, Eden," Lt. Tsuya said strongly. "As soon as Harley Danthorpe gets back. We are all going to investigate the chance that these quakes are artificial."

"Good, sir!" I burst out eagerly. "I'll lead you to the sump, where I saw the MOLE. And we won't have to drain it, sir. I've been thinking it over, and we can dive in thermosuits—"

"Slow down, Eden," he commanded. He gave me a thin smile. "You're making one mistake. I'm not going to begin this investigation in the drainage sump.

"I'm going to begin it in your uncle's office."

We dropped to Deck Four Plus, the three of us, as soon as Harley Danthorpe returned.

We didn't speak; there was nothing to say. There didn't seem to be much panic among the working people of the city. Radial Seven was still rumbling with heavy electric trucks. The factories and warehouses were busy; the air still reeked with the aromatic tang of the great sea's produce, baled and stored.

I guided the lieutenant and Harley Danthorpe up the gloomy stairs between the warehouses at number 88. We marched, in clattering quick-step, down the hall to the door of Eden Enterprises, Unlimited.

I hesitated.

"Go ahead," ordered Lt. Tsuya sharply.

I pushed the door open and we walked inside.

Gideon Park was sitting at a third-hand wooden table in the bare little anteroom, laboriously pecking out something on an old mechanical typewriter. He looked up, saw me, and almost knocked it over.

"Jim!" he cried. "Boy, we've been hoping you'd come!"

And then he saw that I was not alone.

His wide grin vanished. His black, friendly face became blank and impassive. He put the plastic cover over the old typewriter, concealing whatever it was he had been writing, and he stood up with a politely curious expression.

I said awkwardly: "This is Lieutenant Tsuya, Gideon."

"I'm pleased to meet you, Lieutenant," Gideon said politely.

But the lieutenant was having none of that. He demanded: "We want Stewart Eden. Why isn't he here?"

Gideon pursed his lips. "But he is, Lieutenant," he said civilly. "He's in his private office."

"Good," snapped Lt. Tsuya, starting for the inner door. But Gideon moved quickly in front of him.

"I'm sorry," he apologized. "Mr. Eden cannot be disturbed just now. You see, he's asleep."

"Wake him up!"

"Oh, no, Lieutenant. I'm afraid that's impossible. You see," explained Gideon, still polite, still impassive, "Mr. Eden isn't well. His doctor's orders. He's supposed to rest every afternoon at this time. I suggest you come back in an hour or so," he said, nodding politely.

The lieutenant snapped: "You're hiding something, Mr. Park! Get out of my way!"

But Gideon didn't move. Still calm, without any shadow of expression on his broad dark face, he stood immovable in front of the door.

Lt. Tsuya was pale, almost trembling with excitement. For a moment, I thought there was going to be a physical collision.

But then the lieutenant mastered his emotions and, still pale, stepped back.

"I beg your pardon, Mr. Park," he said. "This is a

rather critical matter, and I'm afraid I am acting too hastily. But I am here on behalf of the Sub-Sea Fleet."

Gideon's expression flickered slightly. "The Fleet?" he repeated.

"On a very important investigation, Mr. Park. If Stewart Eden is actually here, you had better get him up. He is in serious trouble, I assure you.

"And for that matter, Mr. Park, so are you. According to Cadet Eden, here, you are involved in some very mysterious behavior—including the possession of a MOLE and what appear to be nucleonic explosives!"

Gideon Park noded slightly. He turned, slowly, and looked at me.

"You followed us then, Jim," he said gently, after a moment.

I nodded. "What the lieutenant says is true, Gideon. I think you had better wake up Uncle Stewart."

Gideon sighed: "Perhaps so, boy. All right."

He turned to the sea-green door and rapped on it.

There was no answer.

After a moment he turned the knob and the door swung open.

The first thing I saw was the huge steel safe in the far corner of the room, and a narrow cot beside it. My uncle's sea-boots stood beside the cot. And on it—

My uncle Stewart leaned on one elbow, looking up at us, his old blue eyes still foggy with sleep.

"Jim!" His sea-faded face brightened suddenly as he recognized me. "Jim, it's good to see you!"

And then he, like Gideon, saw that I was not alone; and the same quick change in his expression happened. It was like a misty veil that was suddenly pulled down between us, hiding what he felt.

When he spoke, his voice was controlled. "Is anything wrong?" he asked.

"A great deal!" rapped Lt. Tsuya. "Cadet Eden, is this your uncle?"

"Yes, sir."

"Then permit me to introduce myself! I am Lieutenant Tsuya of the Sub-Sea Fleet, here on official business."

He scanned the room, taking his time. He scowled

thoughtfully at the safe and said abruptly: "Mr. Eden, the Fleet has reason to believe that you are involved in a scheme to manufacture artificial seaquakes, for financial profit. I warn you that whatever you say may be used as evidence!"

"Oh, so," said my uncle, sitting up. "I see." He nodded blandly, like an old Buddha. He didn't seem very worried. . . .

And he didn't seem surprised.

It was as though he had been expecting this to happen for a long time. He got up and walked slowly to the chair behind his broken-down desk. He sat down heavily, looking at the lieutenant.

"What do you want to know?" he said at last.

"Many things," the lieutenant told him. "I want to know about a MOLE, and about contraband hydrogen devices that your assistant was seen using."

My uncle glanced at me, then at Gideon. Gideon nodded.

"I see," said my uncle at last. "But what has that to do with me?"

It was a most surprising thing for my uncle to say. I had never thought I'd hear him try to shrug off the responsibility for something Gideon had done! But Lt. Tsuya nodded.

"All right then, Mr. Eden," he said. "Let's take up a few things that concern you directly.

"First—" he counted off on his fingers—"there is a question of what you were doing near Mount Calcutta, during a recent eruption in which your sea-car was lost."

My uncle said easily: "Deep-sea salvage is one of my major interests, Lieutenant. We had located a lost ship in one of the canyons below the sea-mount and we were attempting to salvage it."

The lieutenant raised one of his thin black eyebrows. "I'm reasonably familiar with the history of the Indian Ocean. I don't believe there was a major ship lost in the vicinity of Mount Calcutta in the past quarter of a century."

My uncle nodded. "This was an older wreck."

"I see." Lt. Tsuya shrugged skeptically. "Then, if

deep-sea salvage is your business, why did you open this office here in Krakatoa Dome?"

"Salvage is only one of my businesses. That's why the firm name is 'Eden Enterprises, Unlimited.' It takes in any venture I may choose to launch."

"Including stock speculation?" rapped Lt. Tsuya. "I understand you made a million-dollar profit out of the last quake."

"Including stock speculation on occasion, yes," my uncle agreed. "I've been trading in the wealth of the sea for thirty years, Lieutenant. When I arrived here—after the loss of my sea-car on Mount Calcutta—I discovered that security prices here were unduly inflated. I was quite sure that even a minor seaquake would start a panic and force the prices down, and I had no doubt that, sooner or later, there would be such a quake.

"Accordingly, I arranged to make short sales in the market. Does that answer your questions?"

The lieutenant was thoroughly angry now. He snapped: "Not all of them! I have one more question on my mind—and I warn you, I won't rest until it's answered.

"What's in that safe?"

My uncle said sharply: "Lieutenant Tsuya, you're exceeding your rights! I'm a citizen of Marinia. My visa entitles me to the protection of the city government here. If you want to look into that safe, you'll need a search warrant!"

"I've no time for that," said Lt. Tsuya.

"Then I won't open it!"

Lt. Tsuya said seriously: "I think you will, Mr. Eden. For several reasons.

"First, because the quake here night before last was successfully predicted by Cadet Eskow.

"Second, because Eskow and your associate, here, were followed to an ortholytic excavator hidden in a drainage sump under Krakatoa Dome.

"Third, because Eskow and Mr. Park were seen to load the MOLE with trigger reactors for thermonuclear bombs.

"Fourth, because the man who followed Eskow and Park, and discovered the MOLE, is one whose testimony

I don't believe you will hesitate to accept—your own nephew, Cadet Eden."

Sitting slumped back of his desk, my uncle flinched a little from each hammering statement as though it were a physical blow.

His seamed old face flushed with anger. His scarred hands knotted into quivering fists. But at the end, when Lt. Tsuya spoke my name, he dropped his hands into his lap.

"That's enough," he said at last. "You win, Lieutenant. I'll open the safe."

He stood up awkwardly.

He paused for a second, holding the back of his chair as though he were dizzy. But then he knelt, stiffly, and bent to bring his dim eyes closer to the combination.

In a moment the bolts clicked.

My uncle Stewart Eden got painfully to his feet and swung the door open.

I followed the lieutenant to look inside. What we saw hit me like an unexpected depth charge at pressure levels. It had been bad enough to find Bob Eskow and Gideon Park involved in this affair of contraband nuclear explosives and artificial quakes, but now—

The safe was lined with four inches of dull gray lead.

Thick lead bricks were laid inside the door to make a shielding wall.

But the wall was a few inches short of the top of the safe. Light streamed over it, and glittered on heavy golden balls, each one belted with bright straps of stainless steel.

"Contraband atomic fuses!" cried the lieutenant triumphantly. He swung on my uncle, his face furious. "Explain that, Mr. Eden! Atomic triggers—to set off thermonuclear bombs!"

# 15

## The Crime of Stewart Eden

Lieutenant Tsuya closed the door of the lead-lined safe.

He stepped gingerly back from it, with a silent respect for the atomic death it contained. He swung upon my uncle, his face a strange blend of emotions—worry, shock, sadness—and over it all, triumph.

He rasped: "All right, Eden! What have you got to say for yourself?"

"I— I—" My uncle's voice faltered. He stumbled from the safe to the cot and sat down on the edge of it. He shook his head as if to clear it. Then he leaned back weakly against the sea-green wall.

"Those are thermonuclear devices!" cried Lt. Tsuya. "They don't belong in civilian hands, Eden—you know that. They must have been stolen from the Fleet. Why, even the government of Krakatoa has agreed to support the international laws that give the Fleet exclusive jurisdiction over the manufacture and use of nucleonic devices. They're contraband—and you can't deny that they were found in your possession!"

My uncle blinked at him. "I don't deny it," he whispered, so faintly that I could hardly hear.

"And I believe that you have been using them to cause seaquakes!" cried the lieutenant. He pointed a long accusing finger at my uncle. "Do you deny that?"

Painfully my uncle shook his head.

The lieutenant was startled. He glanced at me, then back at my uncle; plainly, he had expected more difficulty. He said, half incredulous and half triumphant: "You admit all this? You admit that you are guilty of a crime so great that there is no name for it—the crime of causing death and destruction by triggering seaquakes?"

"Death?" whispered my uncle. "But there has been no death— no—"

He stopped.

He caught a long, gasping breath.

His sea-worn, sagging face turned very pale and, as though he had been stricken down by a blow, he abruptly slid down on the cot.

He lay with his head hanging limply over the side, breathing hard.

I cried, "Uncle Stewart!" and ran toward him. Simultaneously Gideon leaped to help him too.

But Lt. Tsuya halted us both. "Stop!" he roared. "Stand back! Don't touch him! The man's a confessed criminal!"

"But he's a sick man," Gideon protested gently. "He needs medicine. You'll kill him if you keep me from him now!"

"That," rasped the lieutenant harshly, "is my responsibility. He's my prisoner." He turned to face my uncle, lying unconscious on the cot. Formally Lt. Tsuya droned: "Stewart Eden, by my authority as a commissioned officer of the Sub-Sea Fleet, in the lawful discharge of my duty to prevent illicit manufacture or use of nucleonic weapons in the sea, I hereby place you under arrest!"

My uncle lay gasping, and if he heard the long legal formula or not I could not tell; but while I stood silent Gideon would not be denied. He leaped past the lieutenant to attend to my uncle. Quickly—showing the practice he had had—he put a pillow under Uncle Stewart's head, raising it gently; lifted his feet to the cot; spread a blanket over him. "There," he crooned. "You'll be all right, Stewart. I'll fix your injection now."

"You'll do nothing of the kind!" snapped Lt. Tsuya. "He's my prisoner now!"

Gideon stood up and turned to face the lieutenant.

I do not recall that I have ever seen Gideon very angry; he isn't a man to lose his temper. But just then, angry or not, I was glad that it was the lieutenant who had to face him and not me.

He stood like a giant warrior out of old Africa, and his dark eyes were black as the bottom of the Deeps themselves. He said in a low, deep voice that throbbed and roared: "Stewart Eden has a bad heart, Lieutenant. I intend to give him an injection. If you try to stop me, you'll have to kill me!"

The lieutenant paused for a moment, listening to my uncle's labored breathing, while Gideon brought a tiny hypodermic from the desk and began to roll up my uncle's sleeve.

Then Lt. Tsuya said: "Very well. Give him the injection." And he glared at me.

But by that time it was already done. With deft black fingers Gideon had stabbed the tiny needle into my uncle's lean arm. He pushed the little piston gently home. He drew the needle out, and swabbed away one bright drop of blood.

It took time for it to have its effect.

We all stood there, ringed around my uncle, while he lay gasping under the blanket. Gideon knelt beside him, murmuring to him. My uncle's face looked pinched and bloodless under a film of perspiration.

"You'd better keep him alive!" Lt. Tsuya snapped at Gideon. "We've got a lot of questions to ask him. Stolen reactors—making seaquakes for private profit—I can't imagine more shocking crimes! And this from a man who has been held up to the world as a sort of hero! I want him alive, Park!"

Gideon looked up at him and said softly: "So do I."

He stood up. "It'll take a few minutes, Lieutenant," he said, "but I believe he'll be all right now. When he wakes up, I want you to listen to what he has to say."

"I will!" barked the lieutenant grimly. "You can count on that. But I warn you, I'm not going to believe whatever lies he might cook up!"

"Suppose they aren't lies?" Gideon asked gently.

The lieutenant shrugged.

I cut in at that point. My voice had a dry catch in it,

but I couldn't help speaking—I had waited too long, too long, everything I knew told me that I had waited too long. This was my uncle, Stewart Eden, the greatest man in the world! Or so I had thought as a boy—and so I still believed, in a manner of speaking, now!

I said: "Lieutenant, give him a chance! You don't know my uncle. I do! He couldn't be guilty of any of these crimes! It simply isn't possible. There is some explanation, I guarantee. There *has* to be. Don't make your mind up now! Wait and hear what he has to say when he wakes up!"

The lieutenant looked at me for a moment before he spoke. I could see how worn out he was. Why, I'd had little enough rest, the past few days, but Lt. Tsuya had had none at all, barring a cat-nap on the quake station cot. Worried, worn—and more concerned about my uncle than I realized.

He said in a low, toneless voice: "Cadet Eden, you carry family loyalty a little too far. I know enough about your uncle to know that he was a great and respected man—once. But what does that have to do with the present situation?

"After all, Eden—you heard him admit his guilt!"

It was a crushing blow; I had no answer.

Perhaps Gideon did. At any rate, he started to speak—

But he never had a chance to finish what he was going to say. There as an interruption. I felt myself suddenly unsteady on my feet, flung out an arm in surprise to catch hold of a chair to steady myself, glanced around at the others. . . .

And found identical expressions of surprise on every face. Each one was staggering slightly.

Then surprise became certainty. There was a great rumbling sound out of the deep rock that underlay the city— a giant, complaining basso-profundo groan. The big safe shook itself gently and rolled out to meet me, slowly, carefully, as if unsure of its welcome. The vibration grew, tingling the soles of my feet. A bottle of ink on my uncle's shabby old desk danced tremblingly across the desktop and flung itself shatteringly on the floor. Blue-black ink spattered the cuffs of my dress-scarlet uniform. Harley

Danthorpe took a quick step, missed his footing and fell to the floor.

"Quake!" I cried. "It's a seaquake, ahead of schedule!"

The vibrations must have stirred my uncle even out of his coma—Uncle Stewart was the kind of mariner who would have come back from the gates of Death itself at a challenge like that. He pushed himself groggily up on one elbow. "Quake," he whispered. "Gideon. . . ."

Gideon looked at him and nodded. "That's right, Stewart," he said gently. "Right on schedule. Now we'd better get out of here!"

"Wait!" cried Lt. Tsuya, clutching at the desk. "What are you talking about?"

"This building," Gideon said grimly. "It isn't going to take much of this! If you hope to bring your prisoner in alive, Lieutenant, you better get us all out into Radial Seven!"

The floor was dancing crazily under us now. It wasn't a major quake—not yet; Force Three or Four, I estimated, in the split-second of time I had for such things. But it wasn't by any means over yet. It could well build up to the Force Ten or Twelve that we ourselves had predicted . . . and in that case, it would all be over!

A gargling sound came out of the emergency P.A. speaker on the wall:

"Attention all citizens! Attention all citizens!" it rasped. "This is a Quake Alert! All routine precautions will be put into effect immediately. All safety walls will be energized. All slidewalks will be stopped to conserve power. All public ways will be restricted to official use only."

It coughed and was silent as the power was turned off.

"You hear that?" Gideon demanded. "Come on, Lieutenant! Let's get out of here."

But it wasn't that easy.

The floor shuddered lazily under us again, and the safe, that had minced daintily out into the middle of the floor, now wheeled itself with careful decorum back to the wall once more. Back—and a little more; that safe was heavy; the faint, imperceptible tilt of the floor that moved it gave it enough impetus to crash thunderingly against

110

the wall. Plaster splintered. There was a rattling, rolling bowling-ball clatter from inside it of toppling lead brick and colliding primary reactors—not a pleasant sound! In theory these devices were safe unless specially set off by their own fuses, but it was not a theory any of us cared to count on. If one of them had exploded, caught by some freakish accident in just such a way that it went off—

Why, then, our forecasts would not matter; a Force Twelve quake could strike the city, and no one would care—for we would all be dead, as one sphere triggered the next and all of them went up in one giant burst of nuclear energy, huge enough to demolish the dome entirely!

Gideon commanded: "Grab hold, there. You, Jim! Brace that thing!"

We all sprang to the safe—even my uncle tottered to his feet. Whatever it was that had been in the little needle Gideon gave him, it was doing the trick; his face showed color, his eyes were coming alive. He put his shoulder next to mine and the two of us steadied one side of the safe, Harley Danthorpe and the lieutenant the other while Gideon hastily chocked the plunging wheels with telephone books, the mattress from the cot, whatever was handy.

"Now let's get out of here!" cried Gideon.

The lieutenant cast one glance at the weaving walls of the rickety old structure and surrendered. The building was steel. The foundations were strong enough, the building itself was in no danger of collapsing. But the inside walls—that was another story. Old, untended, under the sea-green paint Gideon had applied, peeling with neglect, it wouldn't take much to crack off the plaster or drop pieces of the ceiling on us. Gideon was right. The only thing to do was to get out into Radial Seven, where we would be safe as long as the Dome itself was safe.

The P.A. speaker hiccoughed and crackled into life again as we were hustling out the door:

"Attention all citizens! Attention all citizens! Here is a message from the mayor! There is no reason for alarm. Repeat, there is no reason for alarm. Our safety devices are holding up well. The mayor expects no casualties or

111

serious damage. The Quake Alert will be lifted as soon as possible. Repeat—there is no reason for alarm!"

"But I'll bet he's alarmed, just the same," panted Gideon over his shoulder, and turned his head to wink at me. It was like old times! I felt a sudden thrill of warmth, remembering the dangers Gideon and I had faced, remembering all the tight spots we had been in, and how we had met them. Artificial quakes—contraband nuclear explosives—why, these things didn't matter! In that moment I was absolutely sure that nothing mattered, except that I was with my uncle and Gideon Park; they would explain everything, they would clear themselves, it was only a matter of waiting and having faith. . . .

In that moment.

But then—something happened.

We came to the street exit, looking out on Radial Seven—now filled with scurrying, hurrying figures, seeking shelter, racing to protect their homes and goods. But there seemed to be no damage. Lt Tsuya whispered fervently: "If only there isn't another quake—"

And my uncle said clearly: "There will be seven more."

"*Seven.*" The lieutenant whirled to face him, his expression grim and contorted. "Then you admit that—"

But he never finished his sentence.

The old building had been vibrating in the residual stresses of the quake; and it was not only the inside walls that had been neglected. An ornate old cornice, set high over the doorway, crackled, sighed, trembled on the verge —and came down.

"Jump, Jim!" snapped Gideon's voice like a whip. I jumped—not quite in time. The cornice came down as I plowed into Harley Danthorpe and the lieutenant. It was false, ugly—a miserable old-fashioned thing; but fortunately so for us, for it was only plaster, not the granite it pretended to be. Even so it caught me on the shoulder. I went head over heels with Harley and Lt. Tsuya. There was a sudden shouting commotion.

And then I blacked out.

And when I woke up, there was Lt. Tsuya, pinned by the legs, screeching like a banshee. "They got away, they got away!" he howled. "Murderers! Traitors! Stewart Eden, I'll get you if it's the last thing I do on earth!"

And Gideon and my uncle, in the confusion, had got clean away.

By the time we got the lieutenant free and tried to get in touch with the Dome police, many precious minutes had passed; the police had enough to do, coping with the Quake Alert; they weren't interested in crazy stories from Fleet officers about contraband atomic fuses and man-made seaquakes.

Lt. Tsuya turned to me bitterly. "All right, Cadet Eden!" he barked. "What do you have to say in defense of your uncle now? He's run away. As far as I'm concerned that proves his guilt!"

I had no answer at all.

**16**

# The Intruder in Station K


Krakatoa Dome had taken a pounding. But there was plenty of reserve strength to meet it; the city had been shaken up, but no more.

We finally managed to get a detachment of Sub-Sea Marines up from Fleet Base to take charge of the nucleonic fuses in my uncle's safe, and ourselves hurried back to the Base and to Station K to check the results of the quake.

"Force Four," said Lt. Tsuya, frowning. "Odd! More than that, it's amazing! We simply *can't* be that far off in our forecast."

Lt. McKerrow, red-eyed, surly from lack of sleep—he had been single-handed in Station K all the long while we had been away—snapped: "See for yourself, Tsuya. I guess we blew that forecast!"

But Lt. Tsuya was not convinced. "Get the geosonde crew out," he barked. "I need a new sounding. Check the instruments, start a new set of charts—I want a forecast within thirty minutes. Becaue I don't think that that was the quake we forecast!"

Sleep. It was the thing I wanted most in the world. But there was no time for it. Exhausted as we were, Lt. Tsuya was right; we had to know what was coming next. If it was true that the most recent quake was man-made, then there was every chance that the big quake, the one we had spotted coming up in our charts, was yet to come.

Force Four had been only a teaser . . . if the big one hit us, lack of sleep wouldn't make any difference at all!

While I was spotting in the converted readings on the sonde run a detachment of Sub-Sea Marines marched in. The commanding captain clicked his heels and reported formally: "Lt. Tsuya, we are bringing in the nuclear devices you found for storage here. Base Commandant's orders."

"Here?" repeated Lt. Tsuya, dazed. Then he rallied. "Get those things out of here!" he yelled. "Don't you think I've got enough on my mind, without a bunch of loose atomic bombs cluttering up my station?"

"Sorry, Lieutenant." The Marine captain was faintly amused. "Commandant's orders." Then he unbent enough to add: "After all, in unsettled quake conditions you can't expect him to leave those things anywhere inside the Dome. They might go off!"

We looked at each other as the detachment of Marines began staggering in under the weight of the heavy golden balls.

But there was logic and truth in what he said. Here, at least, we were down in bed rock. Station K was likely to be the first and most permanent casualty of a really severe quake—but it would be drowned out, destroyed by flooding, much more probably than by the force of the quake itself. And flooding wouldn't set off the nuclear fuses, while a shock well might.

We continued with our work, and as the last of the Marines came in with their deadly cargo I caught a glimpse out of the corner of my eye of a black-robed figure in a clerical collar.

I sat up and stared.

"Father Tide!" I cried.

"The same," he nodded. "Hello, Jim. Good evening, Lieutenant Tsuya. I trust you won't object to my breaking in on you like this."

Lt. Tsuya got up from his stool at the forecasting table and wrung Father Tidesley's hand.

"Believe me, sir," he said, "nobody could be more welcome. You see, our forecasts—"

"I know," said Father Tide, almost cheerfully. "Oh, yes. I know. You forecast Force Twelve and had to settle for Force Four, eh? But you doubt that the qauke you got was the one you had forecast.

"Well, I think you're right. And if you don't mind, I'll help you check out the figures."

"Certainly," said Lt. Tsuya. "We can use all the help we can get."

By then I had my converted figures plotted on the charts; Harley Danthorpe had completed his microseismometer readings; we were all ready to begin.

We began our individual computations, all of us—the two lieutenants, Harley Danthorpe, Father Tidesley and myself. It wasn't hard, for I think that each one of us knew the answer before we began.

Father Tide was the first to finish. He laid down his pencil, nodding slightly, and waited.

Then Lt. Tsuya looked up. "I make it Force Ten," he said.

"Force Eleven is what I got," spoke up Harley Danthorpe.

Father Tide agreed. "But we are all agreed on one thing, eh, gentlemen? And that is that a very severe quake is still ahead of us, probably not more than twelve to twenty-four hours away. Is that correct?"

We all nodded.

"Which," he droned in professorial style, "proves that the recent quake is not the one you forecast.

"Which leads me, at least, to believe that it was man-made—probably by Stewart Eden, and those working with him."

Lt. Tsuya nodded.

Lt. McKerrow nodded.

Harley Danthorpe, glancing at me, said almost inaudibly: "That's the way it looks."

And I—

I don't know what I would have done.

But I was spared the necessity. For on that instant, without warning, the second quake struck.

Maybe it was less severe than the first. The instrument readings showed Force Four, but barely; but perhaps it was only our location. Buildings sway and amplify a quake's vibrations; down in Station K we were deep in

116

solid mother rock. But at any rate the grinding, roaring shudder only made me queasy for a moment, and none of us lost our footing.

But Lt. Tsuya, as soon as he had caught his breath, roared: "That settles it! Those maniacs will bring the dome down on top of us yet. Father Tide, I'm going to the City Council to demand instant evacuation. Do you want to come along?"

Father Tide said soberly: "Try to keep me away."

Once again we left Lt. McKerrow, red-eyed, in sole charge of the station, while Lt. Tsuya, Father Tide, Harley Danthorpe and I hurried up to the city hall. There was raw terror in the streets of Krakatoa Dome now. Damage was still astonishingly light, but the wreckage of public morale was visible on every face. More than once we had to detour and find another way of crossing a radial or getting through a congested central square, as milling mobs blocked our way.

But we made it.

And the council—fewer than half of them present; perhaps they had decided on personal evacuation in spite of the brave face they presented to the ordinary citizens of Krakatoa Dome—was a shouting, yelling catfight more than a sober parliamentary meeting. Each member seemed determined to outshout every other; the accusations hurled around that room ricocheted and drew blood from every person present.

Barnacle Ben Danthorpe was there, rasping: "You're the mayor, Bill! Shut these lubbers up so we can hear what the Fleet boys have to say."

And the mayor, pink and perspiring under the colorful murals of sub-sea life, murmuring: "Gentlemen, gentlemen! This is a crisis. We must all be calm. . . ."

And the other council members, squabbling among themselves—

Father Tide took one look around and then, like Daniel entering the den of beasts, walked gravely to the front of the council chamber. He picked up the mayor's gavel from the floor, bowed courteously to His Honor, rapped lightly on the podium and said, in his soft, clear voice, "Order!"

Magically the hubbub stopped.

Every face turned to look at him.

Politely Father Tide bowed his thanks. He said gently, "Lieutenant Tsuya has something to say to you. Please remain quiet until he has finished."

The lieutenant needed no urging. He bounded forward and, in few words, told the council the exact situation. "We don't know how many artificial quakes are yet to come," he finished. "We have reason to believe there may be at least half a dozen more. But one thing we do know—the big one hasn't happened yet.

"When it does, it is the end of Krakatoa Dome."

"Thank you." Father Tide nodded politely to the lieutenant. "And now, gentlemen," he said clearly, "it seems to me that there is only one thing to do. With His Honor's permission—" he bowed to the pink and unhappy man slumped beside him—"I shall ask you all to vote. The motion is to evacuate every possible human being from Krakatoa Dome at once. All those in favor, please raise your hands."

Hypnotized, nearly every hand in the room went up— even the mayor's, even Harley Danthorpe's and mine, though we certainly had no vote in that assembly!

But a loud, harsh voice cut in.

"Wait!" bellowed Barnacle Ben Danthorpe, lunging forward. "You're out of order, Father Tide! You have no place here!"

Father Tide turned to meet him. "I ask your pardon," he murmured, still polite, still calm. "It seemed to me that a vote needed to be taken."

"Vote?" sneered Danthorpe. "Oh, sure. Why not? Take a vote. Decide to evacuate Krakatoa Dome! And then, for the next fifty years, not one single piece of property in the whole Dome will be worth a holed sea-penny, because every investor will be scared off. 'The Dome they keep evacuating,' they'll think—and buy elsewhere.

"No, Father Tide. I don't care who you are, you aren't going to ruin my investments in Krakatoa Dome!

"As for you lubbers—go ahead and vote. Go ahead! But remember, every man who votes in favor of evacuation is going to have to answer to me!"

There was a moment's silence.

Then, as though nothing had happened, Father Tide said softly: "All those in favor, please raise your hands."

Two hands went slowly up—three—then one of them came down again, and another. And then the third.

There was not one single vote for evacuating the Dome, in spite of everything.

Father Tide sighed.

He laid down the gavel, very quietly, before him. He bowed to the mayor.

He said:

"May God have mercy on your souls."

The third quake hit us as we were almost back to Fleet Base.

"Force Four," whispered Father Tide, clinging to a slidewalk rail with one hand and bracing Lieutenant Tsuya with the other.

The lieutenant pulled himself erect. His face was haunted. "Yes," he said, "Force Four. Always Force Four! Can't they give us the final blow and get it over with?" His voice was thin and tight; he was on the ragged edge of hysteria.

"Calm yourself, my boy," advised Father Tidesley. He stood up experimentally, and then released the railing.

"The worst is over," he said. "And now I must leave you."

"Leave us?"

Father Tidesley said wearily: "I'm afraid we've done everything we can do here in Krakatoa Dome, Lieutenant. It's time for me to board my sea-car and go out into the deeps. This is not the epicenter of the quake, you know. You've seen it on your own charts. I'll go out, as close to the epicenter as I can, and make measurements. . . . Make measurements. . . ."

He said forcefully: "I only wish there was something I could do *but* make measurements!"

And then he passed a hand over his face. "Naturally," he said, "I will take as many refugees with me as my sea-car will hold. But I fear it will be a long voyage to a safe harbor if the Dome fails."

Lieutenant Tsuya stood up and saluted formally.

"Cadet Danthorpe," he rapped, "you will escort Father Tide to his sea-car. Good-by, sir."

"Good-by," echoed Father Tide. He shook Lt. Tsuya's hand, then mine. He said one thing to me. It didn't seem to mean anything to me at the time, but I know what it meant to Father Tide; it was a general injunction, a rule for action in every case. He said: "Have faith."

And later it meant something very particular in this particular case, as well. Have faith. I should never have lost it.

As we were entering the Fleet Base approaches, Lt. Tsuya gripped my shoulder. "Look!" he cried.

We were at the Fleet landing basins. There were viewports in the Dome, and through them—

The Fleet was coming in.

In clouds and clusters, scores of sub-sea vessels of the Fleet were homing in on Krakatoa Dome. Whatever the mayor and city council might vote, the Fleet had its own orders, and was moving in to put them into force. We could see half a dozen squadrons, drawn in by radio and microsonar from their cruising ranges, vectoring in on the Dome. Not enough. Not nearly enough. I remembered the figures: More than half a million citizens would remain trapped in the Dome when the great quake struck, no matter what steps were taken toward evacuation in the time that remained. But oh, what a great sight that was, to see those lean, long, edenite-armored ships, shimmering in the pale light of their hulls, coming in toward the Fleet base!

But it was not enough, as I say.

Wearily, almost beyond hope, we went back to Station K to make more readings and more forecasts.

Canned dance music was on the Dome P.A. system— canned dance music and reassuring statements from the City Council. In disgust, Lt. Tsuya finally turned it off.

We had completed another forecast, and what it showed was the same as always. The time varied slightly, the exact amplitude of the quake was off a few points—

But the big quake had yet to strike. All our forecasts agreed.

The shocks we had already suffered had damaged our instruments. There was no help for that; they had to be built to record the tiniest movements of the rock, and the severe jarring of even a Force Four shock was bound to knock them awry. Yeoman Harris, with a hastily gathered crew of instrument technicians, was busily checking and readjusting them while we made our forecasts.

When we were through, Lt. Tsuya demanded: "What about it, Harris? Is everything working right now?"

The yeoman scratched his head. "I'm not sure, Lieutenant," he admitted. "Everything checks out, but— Well, see for yourself."

Lt. Tsuya trotted over to the microseismograph. He took one look, then blazed: "Ridiculous! You've got something wrong here. These readings—"

Then he paused.

He stared for a long time at the microseismograph trace, frowning. Then, in a different tone: "McKerrow. Eden. Come and see what you make of this."

We hurried over to look.

The amplitude and distance trace was all wrong to begin with. It showed a small, steady, nearby vibration— too rapid and regular to be a rock movement, too strong and powerful to be any machine vibration. That was preposterous; no such vibration should exist. And then the direction shown—why, that was utterly out of the question! For the epicenter of this little disturbance was not down in the magma or at the plotted faults—it wasn't down at all—it was, if anything, up *higher* than Station K itself!

McKerrow said bluntly: "The machine's all wet. Get busy, Harris. You've messed it up."

"No, wait," said Lt. Tsuya. He scowled. "Watch the direction vector," he commanded. "It isn't constant. I've seen it change in the past few seconds."

We watched.

And it was true! Whatever the cause of this small, steady disturbance was, it was not fixed in one place. It was moving, slowly but perceptibly; the readings changed under our eyes; while we watched the direction showed an azimuth change of three or four degrees, and an elevation change as well. The source of the disturbance dipped

121

until it was level with the depth of Station K—then lower; and on the distance and amplitude trace it clearly showed that, whatever it was, it was coming closer.

"What in the world!" cried Lieutenant McKerrow. "Tsuya, have you got a pet earthquake coming to call on us?"

Tsuya shook his head.

He said solemnly: "Unless I'm crazy, I know what that is.

"It's the MOLE! It has come back from the depths— and it's cruising around right now, under Krakatoa Dome!"

For long minutes we stood there watching it—it was incredible! In spite of everything, I had hardly believed that any man-made machine could cruise through solid rock. I had seen our geosondes drop down into basalt, and hadn't believed; I had seen the ship in the pit, and hadn't believed; in spite of all reason and the evidence of my senses, the whole thing had just seemed too crazily ridiculous for belief.

But now—now I had to believe! For nothing else could explain what we were seeing. In the rock beneath us a machine, probably bearing my uncle and Bob Eskow, if not others, was swimming about as casually as a herring in the sea's shallows!

The door to the outer shaft opened and Harley Danthorpe, looking pale and with a haunted misery in his eyes that I didn't understand, came wearily in. "Cadet Danthorpe," he said, with a tragic effort at briskness, "reporting for duty, sir!"

"At ease," said Lieutenant Tsuya absently, glancing at him. Then he stiffened. "Danthorpe!" he barked. "What's the matter with you!"

Harley's eyes were bulging now, staring in horror at something beyond us. He pointed and tried to speak, strangling. "The—the rock!" he cried.

We turned and stared.

Under my hand the microseismograph pen was scratching wildly, trying to record vibrations far huger than it was ever meant to scribe.

In the wall a long crack split open, and water cascaded from it.

Earthquake?

No—there was no earthquake. It was something far stranger! For from that crack came a grinding, tearing, ripping, crunching sound, and the whine of high-speed engines.

A bright gleaming edenite nose poked out of that crack.

Spiral ortholytic drill elements, whirling and coruscating, flared into life behind it.

A shuddering, rattling crash of rock opened a pathway—

And into the lowermost room of our Station K, like a ferret blundering into a rabbit's warren, came crunching the long mechanical body of a Manned Ortholytic Excavator—a MOLE—the stolen MOLE that Bob Eskow had entered in the drainage sump, that had since caused the quakes that seemed to be shaking Krakatoa Dome down around our ears!

# 17

## The Quake Doctors

Lieutenant Tsuya moved fast for a lean little man. He was back in his private office, into his locker and back again with a gun in his hand before the rest of us had recovered from our first astonished shock.

"Stand back!" he cried. "All of you, out of the way!"

The MOLE crept, rattling and whining, a few yards into the room, demolishing the wall charts, shattering the forecast table, chewing a whole rack of blank maps and diagram sheets into confetti.

Then the whirling ortholytic drill elements slowed, dulled, stopped.

The hatch at the top of the little sea-car, now doubling as a MOLE, trembled and rasped. A hand pushed it part way open. It struck against the fragments of rock; the hand shoved hard, hesitated, then banged it three or four times against the loosened rock.

Shards fell. The hatch opened.

And out of it came Bob Eskow, looking like the end of a day of wrath.

"Halt!" rapped Lt. Tsuya, the gun in his hand. "Eskow, don't make a move!"

Bob looked up dizzily, as though he couldn't comprehend what the lieutenant was doing with a gun in his hand. He slid down the ribs of the sea-car's boarding ladder, staggered, almost collapsed and managed to save himself by clutching at the edenite hull. And that was a

124

mistake, because it was hot—blistering hot—smoke-hot, from the friction of the drill elements against the naked rock. Bob cried out and pulled his hand away.

But the pain seemed to bring him back to consciousness.

"Sorry," he whispered, holding one hand in the other, staring at the lieutenant. "We've made an awful mess out of your station, sir."

"You've made a bigger mess than that, Eskow!" rapped the lieutenant.

"I— I—" Bob seemed at a loss for words. At last he said: "Can the others come out of the MOLE, sir?"

"Others?" Lt. Tsuya frowned. "Well, very well," he conceded at last.

With difficulty Bob climbed back up the boarding ladder and spoke into the hatch.

First my uncle, Stewart Eden, appeared—weary, his face beaded with sweat, filthy with grime, but looking in far better health than I had seen him the day before. "Jim!" he boomed, and then caught sight of Lt. Tsuya with the gun. He frowned quizzically, but said nothing.

After my uncle—then Gideon Park. He stood at the open hatch and grinned at us, then turned back and reached down into the depths of the ship to help out the last member of the MOLE's crew.

It was the old Chinese I had seen with Bob!

I heard a gasp from beside me. It was Lt. Tsuya.

"Doctor Koyetsu!" he gasped. The muzzle of his gun wavered and dropped toward the floor. "Doctor, what are you doing here?"

Chinese? Not at all! The "old Chinese" was the Japanese seismologist who had written most of the books on our station shelves—John Koyetsu!

From the moment when Lt. Tsuya saw his own personal hero, Dr. Koyetsu, in the company of my uncle and the others, his certainty that my uncle was a criminal disappeared. It was like the changing of night into day. He turned, without a word, and put the gun away.

And then he said simply: "Doctor Koyetsu, will you tell me what this is all about."

The doctor said wearily: "Of course." He looked

around, a lean, worn old man, pressed very far beyond the limits of his endurance, for a place to sit. Hastily Harley Danthorpe dragged a folding chair across the rock floor to him.

"Thank you," said the doctor, and smiled. He sat.

"You remember what happened at Nansei Shoto Dome," he said abruptly. Lt Tsuya nodded—we all nodded, for it was at Nanei Shoto that the greatest underwater tragedy in history had occurred, when this very Dr. John Koyetsu had issued a wrong forecast and prevented the evacuation of the dome.

"I was wrong at Nanei Shoto," he said harshly. "I have given the rest of my life to finding out why—and to doing something about it.

"The first thing I did," he said, "was to work with Father Tide, for the Fordham Foundation—where we designed the geosonde, and later this MOLE." He patted its cooling flanks. "As you know, with the help of the sondes, we have been able to forecast quakes much more accurately than ever before."

"I'm not so sure of that," I said bitterly—and then hurriedly apologized for interrupting. But Dr. Koyetsu smiled.

"Your forecasts were wrong for a good reason, Jim," he said. "We made them wrong.

"For mere forecasting is not enough. I determined to find a way not only to *predict* quakes far enough ahead to minimize damage . . . but to *prevent* them. And the way to prevent them turned out to be—the creation of artificial quakes. Small ones. Timed just so, occurring in just such a place, that they would relieve the strain in the mother rock that was building up to a great devastation—and release it in small and harmless quakes. Such as the ones that you have seen here in Krakatoa.

"For we created them, the four of us."

The news shook us more than any of the quakes had. Lt. Tsuya's face was furrowed with perplexity; Harley Danthorpe stood stunned, his eyes open wide; Lt. McKerrow shook his head endlessly.

But I—I was exultant!

"I told you!" I burst out. "I told you my uncle couldn't

be involved in anything dishonest or wrong. You should have believed me!"

Lt. Tsuya said harshly: "One minute, Eden! I grant you that Doctor Koyetsu's word goes a long way with me, but there are still a lot of questions that have to be answered for my satisfaction. You can't talk black into white—and your uncle has already admitted, for example, that he made a million dollars out of the panic from the first quake. Not to mention his possession of nuclear explosives!"

"But I think I can explain it all," I said excitedly. "If you will just listen! Because I think that million dollars was far less than he had already spent—that the money was used to pay for the big project on which he was engaged."

"And what was that?" barked the lieutenant.

"The saving of Krakatoa Dome!"

My uncle grinned and spoke up. "Good boy, Jim," he said in his warm, chuckling voice. "And how did you think I was going to do that?"

"Why—" I hesitated, trying to remember exactly what Dr. Koyetsu had said, and to fit it in with all the theory of seismic processes which I had been taught right here in this station—"why, I think it would go something like this. This city stands over a dangerous fault. We have been watching the seismic stresses increase along the fault. The only question was when the whole business would go off.

"But if it could be made to go off prematurely, then the buildup would not be complete. Particularly, if the stress could be released a little bit at a time, no one quake would be big enough to do much damage. And the aggregate effect would completely prevent the big, damaging one.

"It would be a matter of trigger forces," I went on quickly—and I saw Gideon's warm eye wink at me, and knew that I was on a level keel—"and in order to trigger the small, artificial quakes, you would use nuclear energy!

"You would use, in fact, the H-bomb fuses we found in your safe!"

Dr. Koyetsu, smiling and nodding, droned in professorial style: "Exactly right, Cadet Eden. Accumulated crustal tensions are relieved by a series of controlled minor quakes released by nucleonic explosives."

And—"Go to the head of the class, Jim!" boomed my uncle.

But it wasn't quite enough for Lt. Tsuya.

He was convinced, there was no doubt of it. It was impossible for him to doubt Dr. Koyetsu, not to mention my uncle. But he was also an officer of the Sub-Sea Fleet, with a duty to do; and part of that duty was that he should enforce its regulations.

"That leaves three questions," he barked. "Where did you get a MOLE? Where did you get your nucleonic explosives? And, most of all—why was it necessary for you to keep it all a secret?"

My uncle grinned and wheezed: "You should be able to answer that last question." He sat down, color flooding back into his face, his hollowed blue eyes filled once again with their old unquenchable fire. "Secrecy? It was absolutely essential that this operation be carried out in secrecy. What could we do—go to the city council and say, 'Please, gentlemen, we have an idea that we might be able to prevent earthquake damage to the dome. Of course, we'll have to *start* a couple of earthquakes to do it.' Should we have done that? Put it this way. Would *you* have done it, remembering what difficulties you yourself had in trying to deal with a council dominated by Barnacle Ben Danthorpe?"

Harley Danthorpe flushed but said nothing. Lt. Tsuya frowned thoughtfully, then nodded: "Very well," he said. "What about the other questions?"

My uncle said forcefully: "We did what we had to do to save lives!

"This all began a year ago, when Doctor Koyetsu came to me at my home in Marinia. He had kept his eye on the Krakatoa faults. He knew that there was danger here— that sooner or later there would be a major quake, Force Ten or greater, and that that would be the end of Krakatoa Dome.

"And he was determined, for reasons we all know, to prevent any more loss of life through the destruction of an underwater city." My uncle glanced sympathetically at Dr. Koyetsu. "Can you blame him?"

"But why did he come to you?" demanded Lt. Tsuya. "Why not go to someone here in the Dome?"

"Ah, but he did," said my uncle softly. "He went first to see Mr. Danthorpe. I imagine you can guess what Mr. Danthorpe said. We don't want to wreck the prosperity of the dome with crack-brained nonsense, he said, and how did Koyetsu know the thing would work—and lots more.

"And he didn't forget to remind Doctor Koyetsu about what had happened at Nansei Shoto. So he turned him down cold. Refused to let him try out his scheme, and in fact threatened him with arrest if he ever appeared in Krakatoa Dome again."

"He did offer to let me stay on one consideration, Stewart," reminded Dr. Koyetsu.

My uncle nodded. "Oh, yes. He offered Doctor Koyetsu a job—forecasting quakes, to give him the inside drift on quakes that might affect the stock market. Koyetsu took it as an insult at the time. But I don't mind telling you that the idea turned out to be useful to us later.

"Because then John Koyetsu came to see me. He told me his fears about Krakatoa, and his hopes that the quake might be averted—not only here, but everywhere—by the application of his technique.

"At first I was skeptical. Don't blame me too much for that; remember that even Father Tide had been skeptical at first. But Doctor Koyetsu convinced me, and I took a chance. After all, that's been my life—taking chances, for the sake of developing the riches of the deep water.

"The question was, How could I help?

"My health was not too good. It still isn't, I admit, though I think the worst is over! I didn't have much money at the time—and money was needed, great quantities of money; the MOLE cost nearly ten million dollars. And I didn't have the nuclear explosives we needed.

"But I got them!" he cried.

"I got the money, as you know—by speculating on the stock exchange, on the basis of John's forecasts.

"And for the nuclear explosives—why, I remembered the wreck of the *Hamilcar Barca*."

"*Hamilcar Barca?*" Lt. Tsuya looked puzzled. Then he

said, doubtfully: "Oh, was that the one— It was a long time ago, when I was only a baby. But wasn't that the ship that sank in the early days, before you invented edenite armor? And it carried a cargo of—"

"Nuclear fuses!" said my uncle triumphantly. "You've got a good memory, Lieutenant! *Hamilcar Barca* went down near Mount Calcutta thirty-one years ago. And after twenty-eight years, the cargo of any foundered vessel belongs to the man who salvages it. That's the law!

"So I decided that that man was me. What was more, there was work to be done around Mount Calcutta. John had predicted a severe quake there, and he was anxious to test his theories. Well, I got the cargo—and John's theories tested out beautifully—but we ran into trouble." He grinned. "But we escaped, though my old sea-car was a total wreck."

My uncle sobered. "Then Doctor Koyetsu rescued us in the MOLE, with the cargo. And we came here to Krakatoa Dome. We hid the reactors in the drainage sump, along with the MOLE itself, until the time was right to put John's theories into practice.

"That time came four days ago. And the rest of the story you know."

John Koyetsu called urgently: "Stewart! The time—"

My uncle hesitated and looked at the station clock. He nodded gravely.

"Brace yourselves, gentlemen," he said.

There was a silence. Seconds passed—a minute. Lt. Tsuya started to speak: "What are we waiting for? Is it—"

"Wait!" commanded my uncle. And then, almost on cue, we felt it.

The rock shuddered beneath us. A distant awful howl of quaking seismic masses sang in the air. Even in the station we felt it, and clutched, every one of us, for whatever would help us stand.

"The third quake!" cried my uncle over the din. "And there are five more to go!"

Beneath us, the tormented rock was still moaning.

The floor of the station pitched and shuddered.

The ortholytic elements on the nose of the MOLE quivered and spun slowly, twisted by the racking movements of the earth, looking queerly as though the MOLE

130

itself were protesting against the effects of the quake it had itself caused. Rock exploded out of the roof.

And from widening fissures a cold salt flood poured into the station.

**18**

## Grave Down Deep

There was a sudden thumping roar from the tunnels outside. For a moment I was startled—could it be a fresh quake, so soon on the heels of the last? But it was not. It was the drainage pumps, automatically springing into action to suck away the brine flooding into the station.

They were big enough to handle the job; the station would not drown, not yet, though the quake had cost us half our remaining seismographs and split a long crack down the wall of the main tunnel. Dark water trickled out of the splintered stone.

Lt. Tsuya demanded harsly: "Was that one of your artificial quakes?"

My uncle nodded. "Dr. Koyetsu's program calls for eight triggered quakes, in a diagonal line downward against the fault plane. We set four of them. That was the fourth."

"And the other four?"

My uncle said quietly: "Those still have to be set."

There was a silence in the station, broken only by the thumping of the pumps outside and the trickle of water across the floor.

Dr. Koyetsu stood up. "The nucleonic explosives from the wreck," he said, "were under water a long time. Some of them are damaged.

"We used all the active ones we had aboard the MOLE. Then we had to come back for more. We went to

132

the sump—Gideon and Bob Eskow went up to your uncle's office—but the store in his safe had been removed. We found out from the superintendent of the building what had happened. The Fleet had removed them.

"And so we had to come here, to get them. We need them!" he cried strongly. "Without them, all that we've done so far is wasted! The big quake will be delayed, yes—perhaps it will be one or two degrees less powerful—but it will come.

"And Krakatoa will be destroyed."

Lt. Tsuya took no time at all to make his decision. He was trained as an officer of the Sub-Sea Fleet, and the training wouldn't let him waste a second in trying to explain or justify his previous actions. He had been wrong; very well, now he was right; get on with the job!

He said: "That won't happen, Dr. Koyetsu. The nuclear fuses are right here, in one of the storage rooms. We'll help you load them!"

It didn't take much time. Two of us at a time wrapped slings around the gleaming golden spheres, lugged them down the rocky tunnel to the station, handed them up to Gideon, atop the MOLE. "Keep them coming!" Gideon cried, grinning, and hefted the heavy balls into the hatch, where Lt. Tsuya and Harley Danthorpe, under my uncle's directions, stowed them away. Dr. Koyetsu and Lt. McKerrow made one hauling team, Bob Eskow and I the other.

When all the fuses were stowed away Bob and I stood panting for a second, looking at each other. It was an embarrassing moment, in a way—the first time we had faced each other since the whole mysterious affair had started. And both of us were remembering the harsh and mistrustful thoughts I had had of Bob—remembering them, and wishing they could be put out of the way. But at last Bob grinned and stuck out his hand.

"You're a great detective," he complimented me. "Congratulations! I should have been more careful about being followed—but I honestly didn't think you were that good!"

I said seriously: "I'm sorry, Bob." He grinned. I said:

"No, don't laugh it off. I should have trusted you—and I should have trusted Gideon and my uncle too. But—"

I hesitated. "Well," I confessed at last, "there was one thing I couldn't understand. For that matter, I still can't! I understand that this whole thing had to be kept secret. But why from *me*? If my uncle had to have help in the station here, why couldn't *I* have been the one he came to instead of you?"

Bob said immediately: "Because the trail would have led directly to him! Don't you see that, Jim. The best way for him to conceal his own activities was to involve me in them, and not you. When he came to me, just after we arrived here, he explained the whole thing to me. He told me that you would feel left out, and rightly so— but that he counted on you to understand at the end, when everything was explained. And you do, Jim!"

"I guess I do," I said at last—but I wasn't so very sure! In spite of everything, I wished that I had been able to take part of the work and worry on myself!

But Lt. Tsuya, climbing down the boarding ladder, interrupted:

"I have one more question too," he said. "You made that successful quake forecast because you *knew* what was going to happen—knew that Stewart Eden would cause it. Right?"

Bob nodded. "I guess I should have faked it," he admitted. "But—well, it looked like a good chance for me to show how smart I was! And that wasn't very smart. . . ."

"That's not my question," said the lieutenant, shaking his head. "It was after that. The thing I'm talking about is the geosonde that was stolen from the station."

Bob peered at him blankly.

"That sonde cost the Fleet thousands of dollars," said Lt. Tsuya. "And I want to know what happened to it! I'm responsible, you know."

But Bob shook his head. "Sir," he said honestly, "I can't help you. That's something I don't know anything about."

Harley Danthorpe popped his head out of the hatch of the MOLE.

"All stowed away!" he called. "You're all ready to take off!"

And that's when the fifth quake struck.

I suppose it wasn't any bigger or worse than the others. The wave amplitude was no greater, on the seismographs we still had working. But the sound of it seemed louder, when it came moaning up through the rock to shatter the damp, icy stillness of the tunnels. The vibration seemed more painful.

And most of all—this one wasn't part of Dr. Koyetsu's plan!

My uncle turned white-faced to us and cried: "We've got to get those other bombs planted! We've started something and we have to finish it!"

Rock sprayed out of the cracks in the ceiling and caught him as he spoke. My uncle was thrown to the ground, bleeding from the head and shoulder. Rock rattled against the edenite hull of the MOLE like machine-gun fire. I was hit; Dr. Koyetsu was hit; Gideon was knocked flat, but only a glancing blow that pounded the wind out of him but did no more damage than that.

But Koyetsu and my uncle, they were in no shape to withstand that sort of treatment! Neither of them was young—both had been under immense strain—and now, in a fraction of a second, both were smashed down by falling rock, in a quake that signaled enormous danger for all of us.

Lt. Tsuya gave swift orders, and Bob and I helped get the injured ones to a dry and level place on the chart tables. Bob glanced at me and said sharply: "Jim, you're bleeding yourself!" It was true, but no more than a scratch. A sharp-edged flint had raked across my neck and shoulder; the skin was gouged, but not deeply.

We ministered to the injured ones, while Lt. Tsuya computed hastily. Soundings we had none; seismograph traces were scanty, most of the machines being out of commission from the repeated shocks; but the art of forecasting is more in the mind of the man who does it than in the data he has to work with. Lt. Tsuya threw his pencil across the station.

"Here!" he cried. "Look at this!" He scrabbled up

135

another pencil and quickly charted the position of the focuspoints of the five quakes, the four that had been triggered and the fifth that nature itself had brought upon us. "Look!" Red crosses marked the position of each focus; a dotted red line lay between them. "That fifth quake isn't all bad," he said hurriedly. "It will help relieve the tension—provided the remaining trigger-explosions are set off on schedule. The MOLE must go out again at once! There's less than an hour to get the next blast off—and it will take all of that to get in position!"

My uncle pushed himself off the table. "I'm ready," he said hoarsely, clutching at a chair for support. "John—Gideon. Come on!"

But Lt. Tsuya was pushing him back into a chair. "You're going nowhere, " he said forcefully. "We'll take over now!"

"You?" My uncle blinked at him dizzily. "But—but what do you know about it? John and I are experienced at this by now. It's too dangerous for anyone else to go!"

"And it's plain murder for you!" cried the lieutenant. He stabbed at the chart before him. "Here—and here—and here! That's where the next three shots have to go. What else do we need to know? We'll take Bob with us, if he'll go, and Gideon. And we'll need one more person."

"Me!" I cried immediately. But I was not alone; at the same instant, beside me, Harley Danthorpe stepped forward.

"Me!" he shouted. Then he turned to look at me. "I *have* to go, Jim!" he said tautly.

For a moment the station was almost silent, except for the pumps and the splash of water where the sea was running through widening fractures in the rock. All of us were thinking of the voyage that lay before the MOLE, boring through the earth's crust, miles beneath us, under increasing heat and pressure. Five quakes had gone off, but three remained.

And those three must be placed deeper, where the MOLE would be in greater danger of being crushed by slipping rock, or drowned in molten magma. I remembered how many of our sondes had imploded at seventy thousand feet or less—and now we would have to go far deeper than that!

But it had to be done.

And Lt. Tsuya said at last: "Very well. We'll take you both! Lieutenant McKerrow, I'm leaving you in charge of the station and these two gentlemen. See that they're taken care of."

"Thanks," grumbled McKerrow. Then, eagerly: "Listen, why not take six? I'm sure Eden and Koyetsu can get along by themselves."

"That's an order," rapped Lt. Tsuya. "There'll be plenty of work here. Now—" he glanced behind him, at the gleaming armor of the MOLE and the spiral ortholytic elements that wound around it—"now, let's get going!"

While we were completing the loading and getting aboard ourselves, the emergency speakers, long silent, began to rattle again with quake messages and warnings. It sounded bad, even with the limited knowledge the announcer had been given. He spoke of new cracks opened in the drainage tubes, sumps filling faster than the overloaded pumps could empty them. Plans were being made to evacuate all of the dome outside the edenite safety armor. But there was a grave, worried note in his voice as he said it, and I knew why. Edenite was mighty against the thrust of the ocean's pressure, but without power it might as well have been tissue paper. And there was always the chance of a power failure. A mob in the upper northeast octant had tried to fight their way into the platform elevators and there had been trouble—and fighting meant guns; and with guns the power generators themselves might be endangered.

There was no time to waste!

And then the hatch came down as Dr. Koyetsu and my uncle waved.

At once the sound was cut off.

In the tiny, cramped cabin of the MOLE Gideon took his place at the controls. We stared at each other in the dim, flickering lights—all the light we could have; for the armor and the ortholytic drill elements between them took enormous power, and there was just so much left over for other purposes.

"Let's go!" ordered Lt. Tsuya.

Gideon nodded.

He poised his fingers above the starting buttons, hesitated—then pressed four of them in quick sequence.

The edenite armor began to pulse brightly.

The ortholytic elements began to spin.

The MOLE shuddered and rocked, and then began to move.

The noise was like a giant howling of mad dinosaurs crunching rock; there was never another noise like it; even inside the armor, it was almost deafening.

The MOLE lurched and staggered, and we felt it begin to tilt as, crawling backwards, it withdrew from the hole it had breached in the rock walls of Station K.

We were on our way to the bowels of the earth!

# 19

## Sea of Stone

Lt. Tsuya bellowed over the monstrous racket: "More speed, Park! We've got to get down to the fault level in fifty minutes if we're going to do any good!"

"Aye-aye, sir!" cried Gideon, and winked at me out of the corner of his eye. He was enjoying himself, in spite of everything. I remembered the first day I met him, when he pulled me out of the drainage tubes in Marinia, and all our adventures since; danger was a tonic to Gideon Park.

And for that matter, it had done something to all of us. The knowledge of danger didn't matter; what mattered was that we were in action—we were fighting.

Only Harley Danthorpe seemed silent and worried.

I remembered the strange, tragic expression that had been on his face as he came back to Station K, after seeing Father Tide to the sub-sea quays. The MOLE had erupted into the station at just that moment and there had been no chance to study Harley Danthorpe; but something had been wrong. And something was wrong now.

Bracing myself against the plunge and roll of the ship as it chewed its way through masses of steel-hard rock, I started over to him. But there was no time now either; Gideon Park, bellowing over his shoulder, ordered: "Get the nuclear fuses ready for planting! This old tub has taken a terrible beating. As soon as we get them laid, we want to get out of there!"

So for the next little while there was no time to talk.

139

Each golden globe had to be carefully laid in a discharge port—a tube, edenite-lined, something like the pneumatic torpedo tubes of the old-fashioned submarines. But these ports were designed to spew their contents out into solid rock, not water; each port was designed with a special ortholytic cutting tool mounted at its outer hatch. Lining up and sealing those tools was a complicated job; it was a task that belonged to skilled sallymen of the Fleet, not to us—but we were there. By force of circumstance, we had to do it.

We did it.

But the job didn't stop there. Once the nuclear fuses were in place and the port cutting tool properly readied, there came the task of arming the fuses. The stainless steel bands that girdled them were cocking gears. Painfully—for the years at the bottom of the sea had done nothing to make the old corroded gears work more easily—each set of bands had to be aligned to the precise notch that released the safety locks inside. As long as any one band was a fraction of an inch off dead center, the fuses were on safety; we could fling them as far into hot dead rock as we liked, but only sheer accident would make them explode. And that wasn't good enough. It was necessary to unlock the safeties . . . and, of course, there was always the chance that once they were unlocked the weary old fuses would not wait for the impulse that thrust them out of the discharge ports and the timing mechanism that was supposed to set them off, but would on the instant explode in our faces.

That, of course, would be the end of the MOLE and all of us—permanently. There wasn't a chance that a fragment the size of a pin would survive.

But that, at least, didn't happen.

Two of the spheres were too far gone; try as we would, the bands couldn't be manhandled into place. Gideon's face grew long and worried-looking as, from the controls, he saw us discard them one after another. We had two cocked, two discarded—and only two left. If both of those were defective—

But they were not.

We got the three globes into position not more than two minutes before Gideon, bent over the inertial-guidance dead reckoner, reported that we were at the focus of the next quake.

There was a long pause, while the MOLE bucked and roared and screeched through the resisting rock—

Then—"Fuse away!" roared Gideon. Lt. Tsuya, white lines of strain showing around his mouth, came down hard on the port release valve. There was a sudden raucous whine of highspeed whirling ortholytic elements from inside the port, a clatter of metal against rock as the port thrust itself open—

And the first nuclear explosive was gone.

MOLE had laid her first egg with her new crew; two more remained.

We made tracks out of there.

Fourteen minutes later, exactly on schedule, there was a sudden shuddering moan that filled the little ship, almost drowning out for a second the noise of our frantic flight through the rock. The MOLE felt as if it were some burrowing animal indeed, caught in a ferret's teeth, shaken and flung about as the rock shook in the throes of the quake we had triggered. The lights flickered, went out and came back on again—even dimmer than before. There was a heart-stopping falter in the noise of our drill—if it stopped, all stopped; without those whirling elements we were entombed beyond any chance of help. But it caught again; and the MOLE was strong enough to survive the shock.

"That was a close one!" yelled Gideon, grinning. "Next time, let's leave a little more time on the fuse!"

"Impossible!" rapped Lt. Tsuya at once. "We can't open those discharge ports again! The fuse settings will have to remain just as they are!"

And then he saw that Gideon was grinning at him. After a moment, the lieutenant returned his smile. "I thought you were serious for a moment," he apologized.

The grin dried up on Gideon's face. "It might get serious at that," he said, suddenly cocking his ear to the sound of the drills. Bob Eskow, clutching the hand-brace beside me, said tautly:

"I hear it too! One of the drill elements must be working loose!"

I listened. Yes. There was something; but I wasn't expert enough to know what. Above the banging and rasping there was an uneven note, something like an internal-combustion car with some of its cylinders misfiring; the MOLE seemed to stagger through the rock instead of cutting evenly.

I turned to Bob. He shrugged.

We let it go at that. There was nothing else to do. . . .

The second egg went off on schedule. The second blast caught us and shook us just as hard as the first. But we survived—amazingly, when you stop to think that any one of those fuses contained atomic energy enough to trigger an H-blast big enough to slag a city. But even an H-bomb is tiny compared to the energies released in an earthquake; the bombs themselves, damped by miles of solid rock between us and them by the time they went off, were relatively weak; it was the quakes they triggered that endangered us.

But there was nothing to do about it.

Lt. Tsuya took a pencil and figured feverishly in the wan, flickering light; but he cast it away from him after a moment. "I hoped," he muttered, "that that last quake might have been enough. But I'm not sure."

Gideon called, calm and sure over the racket of the MOLE: "Trust John Koyetsu, Lieutenant! If he says we need eight quakes, then that's what we need."

The lieutenant nodded soberly. Then his pumpkin face twisted sharply. "To think," he raged, "that all this could have been done on time—with extra crews and extra MOLEs to do it—if it hadn't been for that city council! I'm a peaceful man—but I hope they get what they deserve!"

Above the infernal noise came the voice of Harley Danthorpe, and even in that moment we could all hear a note in it that explained all the tragedy and worry in his face:

"You get your wish, sir," he said. "They did."

Lt. Tsuya whirled to face him. "What are you talking about?" he demanded.

Harley Danthorpe's face was entirely relaxed, entirely without emotion. He said, as though he were telling us the time by the ship's clock: "Why, just what I say, sir. They got what they deserved."

For a second his calm deserted him, and his face worked wildly. But he regained control of himself. "My father," he said grimly, "and the mayor. And three or four of the council, too. They're gone, Lieutenant.

"Do you remember sending me to the quays with Father Tide? While I was there I saw it. My father's special sub-sea yacht was there—cost him half a million dollars! It was the pride of his life. He'd just had it overhauled, and for a minute, when I saw it, I thought that he'd given it to the people of Krakatoa, to help in the evacuation!

"But that was wrong. It wasn't that way at all."

Harley's face was pale and stiff. He said, almost too low to hear above the clamoring din: "There were eight men boarding that yacht. Eight, when there was room for fifty! And all the rest of the space was taken up with papers. Stock certificates. Property deeds. Bonds—cash— everything my father owned in the way of wealth that he could bring with him. He was evacuating himself and a few friends, not the people of Krakatoa! I saw the mayor with him. And I saw them close the hatch and go into the locks.

"And I saw what happened, when the outer lock door opened."

Harley gulped and shook his head.

"The edenite didn't hold. When the sea pressure came into the lock, she caved flat. They—they were all killed, sir."

For a moment we were silent.

Then Lt. Tsuya said, his voice oddly gentle: "I'm sorry, Danthorpe. Your father—"

"You don't have to say anything," Harley interrupted grimly. "I understand. But there's one more thing I want to tell you. Remember that missing geosonde?"

Lt. Tsuya looked startled. "Of course."

"Well, sir—I took it." Harley swallowed, but doggedly went on. "My dad asked me to. I realized I broke regulations—by stealing it, and even by talking about it. I—" He stopped himself. He said abruptly: "I have no excuse, sir. But I did it. You see, he was going to have more made, using it as a model, in order to set up his own

143

quake-forecasting service, privately. It was the same proposition he offered Doctor Koyetsu. He—he wanted to make money out of speculation."

For a moment Harley's face seemed as though he would lose control; but he hung on and said grimly: "I have no excuse, and I'll face a board of investigation, if we ever get out of this. But I hope I'll get another chance, Lieutenant.

"The inside drift—I never want to hear of it again! If I live through this—and if I get the chance—I only want one thing out of life. I want to be a good cadet of the Sub-Sea Fleet!"

Lt. Tsuya stood up to his full height. He said harshly: "Cadet Danthorpe! You're that already! And now the subject is closed."

It was a dramatic moment.

But it was broken by Gideon's bellow from the controls: "Look at the time! Hurry it up, you down there—we're in position! Get that last egg out of here so we can head for the barn!"

We had barely time to get out of the way of the quake this time. We were heading up at a steep slant, and making slow going of it as the worn old MOLE fought to keep itself alive. When the shock came we lost most of our lights, and they didn't come back.

But the hull stayed in one piece, though it began to creak warningly.

It was a moment of high triumph. "We've done it!" whooped Bob, pounding me violently on the back. "I never thought we'd make it!"

"We haven't made it yet!" bellowed Gideon. "Bob, come here on the double! Give me a hand with these controls!"

The pushbutton system was gone completely, shocked out of circuit by the last quake. Gideon was fighting to handle the stubby manual levers that were supposed to give emergency control of the ortholytic elements. But it was more than a one-man job; the whirling elements that could bite through solid rock were not to be deflected by a finger's pressure; the best Bob and Gideon together

144

could do was to inch it slowly over, and even then it could not be held.

It was touch and go. The noise grew from merely deafening to utterly overpowering as the tortured drill elements began to lose some of their cutting power and beat raggedly against the naked rock. What lights we had were so few and faint that each of us was only a shadow; I turned to speak to Bob, and found that it was Lt. Tsuya beside me; Gideon's face and Harley Danthorpe's were indistinguishable in the gloom. The heat grew and beat on us as Gideon, desperate at last, cut the air-conditioning units out of circulation to conserve power for the drills and the armor.

Minutes passed.

Our instruments showed that we should by now be at the very brink of Station K, almost where the MOLE had erupted hours before. But the instruments were liars; one set contradicted another. Only the inertial-guidance dead-reckoner could be trusted at all, and the power to drive it was growing weaker and weaker, and thus its accuracy dwindled—

And then the drill elements screeched and spun freely in the nose.

"We're out of rock!" shouted Gideon joyfully, and each one of us yelled in plain relief. Out of the rock! Then our mission was accomplished! We were—

We were far too quick! For abruptly there was a sudden shattering *clink* of metal. Gideon's face tightened; his eyes turned dark and worried.

"Our armor," he said briefly. "It's cracked." He glanced at the instruments.

Then he turned and faced us.

"We've come out into water," he said tonelessly. "The thermal shock has cracked the armor. The water is cold, and the armor was plenty hot." He hesitated. "But that's not the worst," he said.

"The instruments are right. We're exactly where we aimed.

"We're in Station K—and Station K is flooded."

We stared at each other for a second—but there wasn't time to think about what that meant. Station K flooded!

My uncle—Dr. Koyetsu—what had become of them? If the station was gone—why, then, perhaps the whole dome was gone! Perhaps all of our efforts were in vain; the dome shaken open and crushed flat. . . .

But there wasn't time. No, not a single second.

"We've got to get out of here!" rasped Lt. Tsuya urgently. "If our armor's gone—"

He didn't have to finish.

If our armor was gone, we were naked to the might of the sea. For a time the edenite force-film would hold; but it depended on a carefully designed metal hull beneath it; without that smooth and precision-engineered metal capsule on which to cling, the film of force could not be maintained forever—might go at any second!

And the instant it went—

Three miles of water would stamp us out like insects under a maul.

"Give me a hand!" demanded Gideon urgently. "We've got to find an airbubble somewhere in the rock—heaven knows where! But if the dome is gone—"

And there too, he didn't have to finish. For MOLE was too heavy, too worn, to become a sea-car again; it would never float, not with what feeble thrust remained in its engines. We could only bore blindly through whatever solid mass we could still penetrate, hoping to find air somewhere. It was the tiniest of hopes. But it was all we had.

And, in a matter of minutes, even that was denied us.

For the old MOLE had suffered one shock too many.

The heat made us dizzy and weak; the screaming, pounding thunder of the drills, unbalanced and wild, was plain torture to our ears. We couldn't manage the stubby emergency levers, not with what strength we had left.

Lt. Tsuya was the first to go. I saw him slip, stagger and fall spread-armed to the floor; and for a moment I wondered dizzily what he was doing.

And then I realized—the heat; the air that was now choked with our own exhaled breath, heavy with the chemical reeks of the damaged machinery. He had passed out. It was simply beyond human strength to take more.

Harley Danthorpe fell away from his post at the emergency levers. I staggered dizzily toward them, tripped

146

over something, paused foolishly to look—and wondered what Bob Eskow was doing, sound asleep on the deck. "Get up, Bob!" I cried impatiently. "What's the matter with you?"

And then I heard Gideon's voice. "Jim!" he called, agonized. "Come help me—I can't hold it. . . ."

His voice trailed off.

I lurched toward him, each step harder than the one before. The MOLE did a looping turn, and abruptly I was on the deck myself. Was it the MOLE that had turned, or I? I didn't know. . . .

But it didn't matter.

I was outstretched on the hot, hard metal deck. I knew it was important for me to get up—to do something—to control the ship in its wild, undirected flight. . . .

But strength was not there. The last of the lights went out. I was unconscious.

# 20

## Father Tide's Foundlings

A small-sized Santa Claus in clerical black was saying urgently: "Jim! Jim, boy. Here, take a bit of this for me."

And something acrid and burning was being forced into my mouth.

I sat up, gasping and choking, and looked into the clear, sea-blue eyes of Father Tide.

"Wha— What—"

"Don't try to talk, boy," Father Tide said comfortably, in his clear, warm voice. His face was smiling, the sea-coral cheeks creased with lines of good humor. "You're all right, Jim. You're in my sea-car. We're on our way back to Krakatoa!"

"Krakatoa?" And then it all came flooding back to me. "But Krakatoa is flooded out, Father Tide! We've been there. Water in the quake station, no sign of life!"

He frowned worriedly. But at last he said: "We'll go back, Jim. Perhaps there may be survivors. . . ." But he could not meet my eye.

I stood up. I was in the forward compartment of a sea-car, Father Tide's own sea-car, there was no doubt of that. For every inch of hull wall was lined with his seismological equipment; microseismographs, core samplers, sound-ranging apparatus, everything. This was the little ship in which Father Tide had roamed the world, studying the secret habits of the quake faults, gathering knowledge without which Dr. Koyetsu's principles could never have been developed. I had heard mu~~~ of this sea-car, and now I was in it.

And I was not alone!

Gideon Park bent over me, his broad black face gleaming with a smile like a sunburst. "Jim, you're all right! We were worried. The rest of us came to an hour ago, but you're a stubborn case, boy!"

"Rest of us?" I demanded.

Gideon nodded. "All of us," he said solemnly. "Father Tide was cruising the area—we were just over the epicenter, you see—and he detected the vibrations of the MOLE. The steering mechanism had failed once and for all, but the ortholytic drills were still going—pointed straight up, churning the sea-bottom sludge, with all of us laid out flat inside it. But Father Tide got us out." He nodded grimly. "He's quite a man. This little sea-car was loaded gunnels-awash with equipment and refugees already. You should see the aft compartments! But that didn't stop him. He took us aboard. . . ."

Gideon turned away.

"So we're safe, Jim," he said. "But as for the others back in Krakatoa Dome—your uncle and Doctor Koyetsu, for two. . . ."

He didn't finish.

There wasn't any need to finish.

But everything else was triumph! In our hearts we grieved for my uncle and the fine people of Krakatoa Dome; but if they had perished, at least we had the consolation of knowing that they would be the last, the secrets of the seismic forces that threatened destruction had been mastered, with Dr. Koyetsu's technique the danger was gone. We worked like demons, all of us, in that little instrument-lined cabin—analyzing the readings Father Tide had made, converting his soundings into plotting measurements, drawing our graphs and charts. And—

"It worked!" whooped Harley Danthorpe, brandishing his forecast sheet. "Look what I get! Probable force, zero. Probable time, infinity. And probable error—so small that I didn't work it out!"

"It checks!" cried Lt. Tsuya, his lean face beaming for

the first time in days. "I get the same results. How about you, Gideon? Eskow?"

We both nodded.

The negative gravity anomaly had begun to fall; the strain had been relieved.

Whatever had happened to Krakatoa, the process worked.

We had proved that seaquakes could be forecast; now we had proved that they could be controlled. Now there was no reason for another Nansei Shoto Dome. Even the dry-side cities were safer now. The great tragedies of Lisbon and San Francisco need never happen again.

(But that didn't help those left in Krakatoa!)

We wrung each others' hands solemnly.

All that next hour, while the little sea-car bustled busily back to Krakatoa, we hung over our seismographs and geosonde gear, alert for any vibration in the earth that might change the bright picture we had built up. But there was none. The crustal strain had been relieved, and the earth beneath the city was again at rest. In the aft compartments the refugees sat patiently, their faces grim but determined. They had been told how we had discovered the lower levels, at least, of Krakatoa to be flooded by the hammering sea; they knew how slim were the chances of finding life anywhere in the Dome. And hardly one of them but had left family or friends back there; it was no wonder that their faces were grim. But they were sub-sea pioneers. If the dome was gone, they would build a new dome!

And so, after long, tense minutes, we drew close to Krakatoa. . . .

Father Tide, his voice queerly muffled, cried: "I—I see indications of the edenite effect! That flow! Those electronic pulses in the scanner screens. I—I think the dome is still intact!"

And in a moment we all saw.

Bulking enormous in the abyss, surrounded by a swarm of sea-cars returning to its sheltering ports, the round, palely gleaming shield of Krakatoa Dome stood strong and safe.

The armor had not failed!

Not only had Dr. Koyetsu's triggering technique proved